THE POSTCARD

THE POSTCARD

by Tony Abbott

LITTLE, BROWN AND COMPANY
Books for Young Readers
New York   Boston

Little, Brown and Company

Hachette Book Group USA
237 Park Avenue, New York, NY 10017
Visit our Web site at www.lb-kids.com

First Edition: April 2008

ISBN-13 978-0-316-01172-3
ISBN-10 0-316-01172-X

10 9 8 7 6 5 4 3 2 1

RRD-C

Designed by Tracy Shaw

Printed in the United States of America

To my grandmother
Mary Banyar
1900–1978

THE POSTCARD

CHAPTER ONE

"She died today."

It was the first Wednesday night after school let out for the summer. I had just switched on the television and was searching with the remote — reality, reality, news, rerun, reality — when the phone rang, and my mother answered it.

"Wait, say that again?" I said.

She pulled the phone away from her face and cupped her hand over it. "She died this afternoon. Your father wants you to come down for a few days. You can get a standby flight in the morning."

I hit the mute button on the remote. "Grandma?"

"He wants you there. There's a lot to do."

I kept watching the screen, but my eyes began to unfocus.

My grandmother. A hospital had called two weeks ago to say she had been brought in with a stroke and was in a coma, so Dad took the next plane down from Boston and had been there ever since. I'd never met Grandma. We never saw her as a family, and she didn't travel. Even my father said that when he was young she wasn't around very much, and he was sometimes brought up by other people, which made her seem odd to me.

I had no clue then about how she lived or who she was or what was going to happen to me because of her.

"I just got out of school," I said, glancing up at my mother. "It hasn't even been a week. I really don't want to —"

"He'll call you back," she said into the phone. "Yes . . . I know . . . Ray, I know!" *Click.* "You're going."

We hadn't really talked about Grandma much since she had gone "off," as my mother called it. Dementia-of-the-Alzheimer's-Type, she told a friend on the phone once. I was three or four when that started. Mom said it was sad

2

when this happened to old people. "It really is," she said. But she also said that my grandmother insisted she could fly — that she was "vehement" about it. I could tell the idea of a flying old lady really freaked my mother out. Other times, Dad let it slip that Grandma had called claiming she was in danger and had to escape, or was being attacked by alligators.

"Again?" Mom said. "They really should keep reptiles away from older people."

There was something going on between my parents about Grandma, but I never knew exactly what it was. I think all the talk and the silences embarrassed my dad, especially in front of me, so after a while he didn't talk about her, and neither did we.

One thing I do remember. My dad once received a letter from St. Petersburg where she lived. In it was a photograph of her sitting in a wheelchair in front of a little green house. She looked like a tiny bird skeleton, fragile, bony. She was as thin as nothing.

I remember thinking she would probably die soon. In a few weeks at most. Weeks stretched into months and finally into years. She was eighty-two on her last birthday. Her name was Agnes Monroe Huff.

"What does Dad actually want me there for?" I asked, flipping the sound back on and turning it low. "I don't know how to do anything. Why not you? I can stay with Becca or Mark."

She was already marching upstairs. "I have to fly this weekend for the bank," she called. "You're going down there. I'll get your duffel bag from the attic. Shut that off, Jason. Now."

Gandy Bridge, Six Miles Long, Between Tampa and St. Petersburg, Florida. P-106

CHAPTER TWO

So my name is Jason, and I think my family is splitting up.

When the jet lifted off the runway the next morning, I couldn't stop thinking about me being in the air and my parents on the ground in two different places, and it seemed so obvious that I was amazed it had taken me so long to see it. Hector knew it for I don't know how long. The way he finally said it a couple of years ago was as if he thought I knew it, too.

We were at lunch on Tuesday the first week of sixth grade, comparing notes about who in our homeroom had

had the best summer experience ("Paris with my two uncles," "the doctor said I nearly died," "rafting, and I even saw a bear!" compared to my "lawn mowing" and Hector's "hammocking, because," as he said, "I'm the *hammock king*!"), when I opened my lunch bag, looked in, and pretended to gag.

"Jeez, what is that? Sliced dog brain? Who shopped at the morgue this week?"

Hector peeked into my lunch bag. He wasn't playing along. "Yeah, what do you expect?"

"What does that mean?"

"Are you kidding?" he said. "I mean, I'm always at your house. I see stuff. Can't you tell your family's sort of falling apart? School lunches are a real tip-off."

"What? You're nuts."

"And not even *sort of* falling apart. You actually are. But not all over the place like my cousin's family. What a circus that is, with the probation and the guardian. No, you guys are being pretty neat about it. So I have to say: dude, well done."

"Neat? What are you talking about *neat*? We're fine. You're nuts."

Hector shrugged and stuffed a baby carrot into his

mouth. "Okay. I'm nuts. Mmm. Vegetables. Someone cares for Hecky."

I hadn't looked. I hadn't seen. But after Hector said that, it was all I could see. And I saw it in hundreds of little things. A comment at dinner one night. My dad having an edge in his voice that I had never noticed before. My mother going out and him coming in and calling her name, not knowing she was already gone.

"I was going to go, too," Dad said to me, as if asking me to take sides. "I can stand her parents, you know."

"Sure," I said. "I know."

"I can stand them for a few hours," he said.

"I know."

And her always redoing things he had just done. Restacking the dishes in the dishwasher. Reordering the cake he had already ordered for my birthday because she assumed he didn't remember to do it but didn't check with him to see if he did.

"I thought you forgot" was her explanation.

It made him seem like a loser — *she* made him seem like a loser sometimes. I hated it, but I wasn't sure what to think.

Was she right?

One thing I did know was that Hector was right. We *were* neat. No yelling. No big scenes. Sometimes my father would drink with supper. Not a lot, a beer or two, but he never used to do that. It made him quieter.

It didn't help that he kept sliding from one job to the next while Mom kept getting promoted. She worked in a big Boston bank and a couple of years ago had gotten a huge promotion. While Dad was still figuring out what he wanted to be, my mother had known for a long time, and she was doing it in a big way, especially now that I was going into high school. Mark and Becca were teenagers when I was born. She had waited a long time.

When I went upstairs to her room after Dad's phone call last night, she was ironing a white shirt for me. "It might be fun," she said. "Florida. After the business with your grandmother is over, I mean. Your friends would love to spend a few days or a week there. And kids make friends fast. It's a resort city, you know, St. Petersburg."

"You always say that," I said. "And a week? Who said a week?"

She turned to me. "I can't go right now. It's a busy season coming up. And the St. Louis meeting —"

"St. Louis? I thought you were going to Chicago."

"St. Louis is after Chicago," she said. "That's a lot of nights away from home. But if you're down there, I won't worry about you. Either of you."

"I'll be okay. I have cable, my computer. Becca's only in Brookline if I need somebody."

"Jason, you're thirteen. I can't leave you here alone for that long."

"So I can stay with Hector," I said. "Besides, Florida in the summer? In two minutes I'll be a puddle on the sidewalk. Or do they not have sidewalks yet? Is Florida even a state? Isn't it all submerged, anyway? You know, just, no. I don't want to. No way."

"No way? No way?" she said, slamming down the iron and stepping toward me, looking tired, but her face set hard. "Who do you think you are to say 'no way' to me? Who do you think I do all this for?"

"I don't know," I said. "You?"

She raised her hand as if to slap me, then dropped it. "Shine your loafers, smartmouth, you're going."

She was right. I was a smartmouth. And I had the paperwork to prove it. I was actually named student of the month twice in fifth grade. It all went downhill after Hector crunched his baby carrot.

"So guess what," I told him on the phone from my room. "I'm going to stupid Florida tomorrow. My grandmother died. My dad's there already. My mom's got a business trip to China or somewhere."

"Wow, your mother traveling. That is so new," he said. "Here's some advice. Don't make eye contact with the old folks, okay? Florida is filled with them, and they're always looking for new blood. You know, like vampires."

"But don't they all have false teeth?"

"Ah, my son," he said, "you are learning the ways."

"Yeah. Look. I gotta shine my shoes. Call you from hell."

Looking out the small window, watching the ground pull farther and farther away below me, I wondered if it would actually be that bad, or if it would be worse.

S-58—Oranges Growing at Midway Groves, between Bradenton and Sara...

CHAPTER THREE

Three hours later the jet landed in Tampa. It was only noon, though it seemed as if I'd been traveling for days. The heat hit me in the face when the terminal doors opened on the parking lot. The air was thick, white, and wet. I was completely sticky inside a minute and a half. Even my eyes began to sweat.

Summer in Florida. Yay.

Blinking away the persperation, I looked around and saw Dad hurrying across the sidewalk to me. He seemed shorter than I remembered. More rumpled. Blurry at the edges. Even pale. How could he get pale with so much sun? Had he made eye contact with the old folks?

"Sorry, traffic," he said. "Thanks for coming." He took my backpack and duffel, walked with me for a bit, then dropped them on the ground behind a bright lime-green rental car. He beeped it open.

"Nice," I said. "What is this, the Hyundai Inchworm?"

He tossed the bags into the trunk and snapped down the lid with a laugh. "I'm glad you're here," he said.

"Oh, yeah. Me, too."

He kept his smile. "You'll like St. Pete."

Right. This was his place, after all, his hometown. He had grown up here with Grandma or whoever, which was the whole reason I was down here. I tried to remember her face from the photograph of her in the wheelchair. When I couldn't, I found myself thinking of any old dead skinny woman lying in a coffin. That just scared me.

"I'm sure," I said.

After getting out of the airport (in a completely round-about way, it seemed to me), we drove toward the water. The roads were flat. The buildings were low. Everything was hot, flat, white, and flat. Soon we were on a long (mostly flat) bridge with a hump in the middle like an arching caterpillar.

"This is the Gandy Bridge. That's the second Gandy down there, from the fifties," he said, pointing to a low strip of concrete running alongside the bridge we were on. It stood a few feet above the water on concrete posts. It had old-fashioned street lamps curling over it. "The original Gandy from the twenties was the first bridge between Tampa and St. Petersburg. Six miles long. What we're on now is the latest Gandy."

Gandy, Gandy, Gandy. Maybe it was the latest, but it was jammed. I saw other bridges in the distance with faster-moving traffic.

"Why did we go this way?" I asked him. "It's so slow."

"This is how I always go," he said. Then he added, "Went. When I was in high school."

Looking at him then brought back the business with Mom at the airport that morning. After the ticketing and check-in, I was heading for the security line, when she suddenly took my arm and said "Jason" in a way that made make me stop and look at her.

"Yeah. Mom."

"Your father has . . . oh, this is going to sound . . . uck . . ."

"What?" I said.

"I don't know. Ups and downs. In his life, I mean."

I swallowed and began to feel hot.

"Lots of things that he really doesn't talk about."

"Okay," I said.

"I mean, it's hard for him. Really hard. And it's easy for the rest of us — for me — to not know what to do about it. We're so busy, you know, with things, for that . . ."

"I sort of have to get in line," I said.

She kept holding my arm. "I'm sorry, but . . ." She was looking intently at me. "Jason, I just don't know what to do sometimes. Or what to say to make it better. Do you know what I mean?"

"Yeah, I know," I said. "He keeps stuff inside him. About Grandma. About everything."

She sort of jerked back at that. "Yes. He does."

There was an announcement over the system then, and we were back in the airport from wherever we had just been.

"Okay," I said. "I get it. Really."

When I thought all that was over with and we got to the security area, she said, "Jason, make sure he doesn't drink too much, okay?"

I turned. "What? Mom! How am I supposed to —"

I happened to catch the eye of the girl behind me who was suddenly all paying attention.

"Never mind," Mom said.

"Gosh, Mom!"

"Never mind. He won't drink. I'm sorry. This is too serious."

Too serious.

I turned away from the flat road and looked out the car's side window. The sun stood straight up in the sky, a burning ball of heat.

"Beautiful, isn't it?" Dad said when we neared the end of "the Gandy" and drove onto real land again. The area on either side was thick with scrubby trees and white sand. Here and there brown palm leaves lay scattered, curled and stiff like body parts.

"It's super hot for sure. And flat."

"But this is nothing," he went on, smiling right and left like a tour guide. "What we just drove over is only

Tampa Bay. Soon, you'll see real water. Maybe the day after tomorrow we'll go. After the funeral. The Gulf of Mexico. It's something to see. It's huge."

I hadn't noticed it at the airport with all the diesel exhaust from the buses, and even now it was pretty faint because we had the windows open, but I could smell beer on him. Not a lot, not a heavy smell; he wasn't drunk or anything, but I was pretty sure he'd had something.

"You're supposed to like water when you live in Florida," he said when we stopped at a light. "And sun."

"I don't live here," I said, turning to him. "Do you?"

The light changed, and he drove on without saying anything for a time, then: "No, Jason. No. Just until I sell Grandma's house. Then I'll be back up to Boston."

So that was it. Our family really was splitting up.

RB-8 TIGER AT RINGLING BROS. WINTER QUARTERS, SARASOTA, FLA.

CHAPTER FOUR

My grandmother's house was on a street called 30th Avenue North. All the streets were numbered like that in a huge grid, going both up and down the whole peninsula; kind of boring and confusing.

The house was a one-floor shoe box made of stucco and painted pastel green. It had old flaking windows and a tile roof and a square block of a garage. The hedge next to the driveway was neat on the top, but not on our side, so I guessed it was the neighbor's. The grass in the yard was long.

We pulled into the driveway and got out. While my

dad took my stuff from the trunk, I looked up and down at the other houses, then at Grandma's. It seemed like a normal house, but small, and I was reminded of the last time my parents had talked about it.

"You should sell that place," Mom had said. "It's not far from the water. St. Petersburg is a resort, after all. Don't they call it the 'Sunshine Resort'?"

"City," he said. "The Sunshine City."

"We have someone at the bank who handles relocations. Bonnie could sell it for you —"

"No," he said. "My mom still lives there."

"She should go into a home."

You could see him get mad at that, but he swallowed it. "And not have a house there at all? She has help. She's all right for now."

"Why do we need a place there? I'm not retiring to Florida. It's worth money. Much more than she paid for it. Or whoever paid for it. Not your father. Maybe Mr. Fracker," she said, moving her hands but, glancing over and seeing me, not quite making air quotes around "father."

"Ha, ha," he said coldly, letting it show now.

That was a real dig. Dad's father, a guy named Walter

Huff, had supposedly died long before Mom and Dad got married. Dad had never had much to say about him maybe because he didn't know him, either. But Mom didn't seem to buy it. From the comments she made, I think she thought he'd actually been in prison or something, and that Dad was ashamed of him. Mr. Fracker was a lawyer who said he knew Grandma and who had met Dad a few times over the years. But the lawyer was old and that was a long time ago, and it seemed sketchy, anyway, so who knows?

The less Dad said, the more Grandma seemed to become strange and shadowy and distant. I felt over and over that there was more to tell, but I didn't know who would tell it, and it was never told, anyway. It only got worse as Grandma got sicker and fought more alligators. Mom wanted Dad to close off the subject of Florida, to shut it all down, and never talk about it. His mother, his father, Mr. Fracker, the whole thing. More than all that, there was the splitting up to worry about, too, so I gave up trying to understand it.

Dad unlocked the front door, and we stepped in. It was cooler inside, but not much, and it was stale. My first thought was that he was keeping Grandma in there before the funeral. Was that how they did things in Florida?

"You can have the front bedroom," he said.

While he went through the house opening windows, I looked around. To the left of the front door off the living room were two bedrooms and a tiny bathroom. To the right was a larger room that went from the front to the back of the house.

"That's called the Florida room," he said.

The front and back walls of the Florida room were nearly all windows, the kind with slats of glass you crank open and closed. He cranked them open now. In the room were a desk and chair, a couch, and a long, low buffet for dishes, like we had in Boston.

The kitchen was no more than a hallway from the living room to the back door, and the backyard was small. The lawn needed to be cut there, too. There was a shed in the corner. I wondered if Grandma even had a mower and if Dad would ask me to cut the grass like I did at home. I hoped he wouldn't; it was so unbelievably hot outside.

Cartons were piled in every room of the house, some packed and taped, most empty and waiting to be filled.

"Trying to get it all cleared so we can sell it," he said as the air moved in and the stale smell began to lessen. "Not getting very far. And there are lots of things to fix up. Except for the kitchen tiles. For some reason, they're new. She let a lot of things go."

I nodded. "Well, she was sick."

He didn't say anything right away, then: "She was sick. The whole time, she was sick. So that's why . . ." He set down his keys on a little divider shelf between the living room and kitchen, paused for a second, then said, "Look, Jason."

Oh, not another serious talk.

"Uh-huh?"

"It's just that I have to tell you . . ."

Really, you don't.

"I have to tell you, mainly because somebody might say it while you're here. Not that we'll really meet anyone."

My arms shivered. "Okay . . ."

"My mom, your grandma, was never married."

I think I frowned, not really understanding. "Wait. What? What about Walter Huff? Your father?"

"There was no Walter Huff," he said.

I looked at him, shaking my head. *What the heck does that mean?*

21

"Grandma's father, your great-grandfather, made him up, he made the name up. He had some documents filed, there were a few newspaper articles, things like that. But Walter Huff wasn't really anyone." Dad said this with a kind of snicker. "Not that I've known for all that long. I only found out after the old man died that he created Walter Huff from nothing. Fracker, the lawyer, told me."

"Dad!" I said, shocked. "So who's your father?"

"I don't know. I don't know," he said, turning away and moving things nervously. "There was no Walter Huff, that's all I know. Having a child, like that, outside of marriage like my mother did, wasn't done. We're talking the early sixties. To be not married and have a child? Uh-uh. When I finally got up the nerve to tell your mother, she thought it was completely fantastic. Not about Grandma not being married, but that this man who I thought was my father was a . . . fiction. Unbelievable, really. From then on, she didn't like it when Mr. Fracker came to see me. She thought he was some kind of sketchy guy, criminal or something. She was never convinced he was even a lawyer, or *just* a lawyer. I finally told him to leave me alone. It got to be too much for me, too."

"Well, yeah," I said.

"Right. But that's it. That's the story. Your grandma didn't have a husband. I never knew who my father was. There was a made-up name, but nothing else."

"But how can you even do that?" I asked. "Make someone up? How could *you* not know? Couldn't anybody tell that this guy, Walter Huff, was never around?"

He shrugged. "He didn't have to be for very long. When I was still a baby, he was supposed to have been away on business when he had an accident. So my mother became a widow. It's nutty, but the old man was like that. So they say. He could do that and make it stick. I never met him. He never acknowledged that I was his grandson, of course."

"Make someone up," I said. "That is so bizarre. So that's why Mom always said stuff."

He glanced at the floor, nodding. "It was just one more crazy thing about my mother."

You're telling me! Grandma suddenly seemed stranger than I ever thought she was. What kind of life had she had, anyway? And *Dad*? What was *his* life like?

Dad seemed tired all of a sudden. "So there you are. No murders or mysteries or anything like that. We're talking Florida when I was young. There had to be a husband, and her father made one up. For a little while."

He was talking so much! He never talked like this at home.

So Dad was illegitimate. His mother wasn't married when she had him. I guess I felt a little like Mom did about Grandma flying. Grandma having a baby and not being married is one thing. But that her husband was a . . . phantom? And after so long for some guy to tell you that your father is not your father and is really no one? So nobody knew who my grandfather was? Is?

There were too many questions for me to deal with. Maybe Mom had the right idea. It was too unbelievable. Too strange. Shut it down. Close it off.

"All right, Dad. Thanks for telling me. I'll keep it in mind. Thanks."

He opened his hands and gave me a look as if he expected more. "Do you . . . have any questions or anything?"

My mind was a complete jumble. "I don't think so. I'm good."

I wasn't good. I didn't want to be there. It was so hot. I didn't want to know about anything. So I had a made-up grandfather. So what? I hated the place. I wanted to be back in Boston with the house all to myself.

Air View of St. Petersburg, Florida "The Sunshine City"

CHAPTER FIVE

While my dad moved boxes noisily around, annoyed at me for not asking to know more, I went into the kitchen, checked the refrigerator, and found store-made potato salad, jelly, eggs, and one beer.

It was nice and cool holding the door of the fridge open, until he snapped at me — "Get inside or shut the door!" — and I finally had to close it.

Looking out the screen door, I studied the backyard again. It was a small square, butting up against the back-yard of the house on the next street (31st Avenue North?

29th Avenue South?) and alongside two other backyards. A hedge of flowering bushes and a couple of thick, dense, low palm trees shielded it all around from the neighbors, except on the right side, where the hedge was low and looked into the yard next door.

I jerked back from the screen. There was a tiny white-haired woman in the next yard, leaning in over the hedge, staring at a big open flower on our side. She was about a foot away from it and not moving an inch.

"Is she a statue or something?" I whispered over my shoulder.

"Who, the lady?" said my dad, stopping his work.

"She's gawking into our yard and not moving. Like a garden ornament."

He snickered and said her name was "something like Mrs. Keep or Mrs. Keefe." She had been a friend of my grandmother for a long time. "She takes photographs," he said. "She used to work for the city or something."

"I don't get it," I said. "Which is it? Keep or Keefe?"

He snorted a chuckle. "I never heard it right to begin with. Maybe it's Mrs. Keese. Or even Quiche. She helped me a bit, but she can't lift anything, of course. She did go through Grandma's closet and found some important papers." He pointed to a white carton in the living room. "I haven't gotten to them yet."

"So what do you call her?"

"Ma'am," he said.

The lady moved slightly and lifted a small black box up to her face. That's when I saw that what she had been staring at was not the big flower, but a tiny bird. A hummingbird. It had been hovering inside the flower and now emerged, its wings blurring. The lady tensed. I didn't hear the *click* of the camera, but the next moment she pulled away, and the hummingbird jerked up and off into some other yard. She then stepped backward across her own yard and disappeared into her house.

"You could check the phone book," I said.

"She's unlisted."

"There's gotta be a way to find out what her name actually is."

"Well, it's too late to ask her," he said. "I've been talking to her every day for two weeks. Each time she calls on the phone and says her name, it sounds different. I think it has something to do with whether she has her teeth in or not."

I laughed. "You could look at her mail when she's out."

"You think I didn't try that?" he said, coming up next to me and peering through the screen at her house. "It's not like she gets a lot of mail to begin with, but the moment it comes, she snatches it in. Besides that, she's almost never out. She lives alone and hardly goes anywhere. Meals on Wheels brings her stuff to eat. I tell you, she never leaves."

"That's so bizarre," I said.

He was almost laughing now. "That's St. Petersburg."

CHAPTER SIX

After having jelly sandwiches, we started on the buffet, emptying the drawers of silverware and plates, wrapping whatever was worth saving in newspapers. We did this for an hour or so, not making much of a dent, when he looked up.

"Hey, Jason. I just remembered the obituary is supposed to appear today. Grandma's obituary. Can you run to the store on the corner and get a paper? *St. Petersburg Times.* I stopped delivery last week."

I nodded. "Sure. Any chance to go out in the heat."

He dug in his wallet for a dollar. "It's nothing much. The funeral home helped me write it up. We should have a copy."

I went out into the sun, wilted down the sidewalk, crossed at the corner to the store, pulled a paper from the twirly rack, and paid for it. When I left the store, a long funeral procession was going by. Nice. Was this to prepare me for tomorrow? I saw headlights and black cars far away into the distance, so I couldn't cross the street. I decided to walk back on the far side.

I had just started up toward the corner and was flipping to the obituary page when I felt something hit my shoulder from behind.

"Off."

I turned around. Standing there was a girl around my age in a bright orange T-shirt and cut-offs. She had light brown skin and long black hair. She was holding her rake like a weapon. She had tapped my shoulder with it.

"Off," she repeated.

"Off what?" I asked.

She nodded toward my feet.

I looked down. The toe of my left sneaker was touching the edge of the lawn. "Oh, sorry —"

When I looked up, she had already turned down the side of the house toward its backyard.

"Insane much?" I said to myself. I crossed the street after the last funeral car had passed and was home in less than a minute.

Dad opened the paper to the obituaries, and we read it together.

AGNES MONROE HUFF, 82, of 30th Ave. N., died Wednesday in a St. Petersburg hospital after a long illness. The only daughter of Quincy Monroe, she was a resident of Pinellas County since birth. Her adventurous spirit has flown; her passing will be mourned. Survivors include a son, Raymond, his wife Jennifer, and three grandchildren of Boston. The Brent Funeral Home is in charge of arrangements. Burial is scheduled Friday, noon, at Bay Pines Cemetery.

"Nice," I said.

"Nice? What is that?" he snarled, flapping the paper. "'Her adventurous spirit *has flown*'? God, enough with the flying. Who the heck wrote that? I didn't. Where did it come from?"

"I don't know," I said. "What's wrong with it?"

"She was in pain, that's what's wrong with it. Her whole life Mom was in pain. There was no adventure. There was no spirit. There was a wheelchair. Who would write that? Gosh, the number of times I was kicked out when the doctors came to work on her. Mom was sick. She was sick and in a chair and then she was sick in her mind."

This came out all at once. He made a kind of grunting sound and tossed the paper to the floor, his hands shaking. He started back for the boxes when he glanced at his watch and said, "Never mind. We're already late. We can pack up later. We have to see the agent who'll be selling the house. He called me this morning before you came. Come on. In the car."

S.83—Alligators in Tropical Florida
Sarasota Jungle Gardens   3C-H358

CHAPTER SEVEN

I couldn't see what the big deal about the obituary was, but obviously Dad was angry and had things to say about Grandma, and now after his first bombshell about her he was starting to say them. Maybe because Mom wasn't there to stop him.

He seemed okay by the time we got downtown and even joked about the air conditioning in the real estate agent's office. It was roaring full blast when we opened the door, and he pretended to stagger back out to the sidewalk.

I said I was cool for the first time since the airport.

"Not counting when you opened the refrigerator door!" he laughed.

Good one, Dad.

Randy Halbert was a puffy-faced guy about my father's age, but with a very brown, young-looking mustache. Weirdly, his eyes never met you. No eye contact at all. Dad and I were there for almost an hour, but his gaze kept flicking around the desk between us, out the front window, at his secretary's phone, his shoes, anywhere but at us. Maybe he had a lazy eye and couldn't focus. It was just plain odd.

His hands were fidgeting all over the place, too, checking the position of his pencils, aligning them at right angles to his coffee cup, shifting a little plastic alligator, his stapler, and all the while chuckling under his breath as if he knew some private joke.

That was not only odd, it was annoying.

"I think we'll be able to do a good job for you, and quickly. There's quite a demand for quality little houses like yours," he said, still amused at something. "For people to retire to, own as a vacation home, an investment, for a rental property, to die in, what have you."

Maybe he was right to laugh. *To die in.* That was funny.

"St. Petersburg is called the City of the Unburied Dead. Did you know that?" he said to no one in particular. Now he was just being creepy.

Lying open on his desk was a copy of the real estate section of the same paper I had bought. While he was blabbing on to my father and checking and rechecking his computer, I looked at the picture on the front page of the section. It was of an old, fairly low structure towered over by tall office buildings.

"I thought you'd like to see that," Randy said unexpectedly, smiling at my throat.

"Sorry, what?" I said.

"The Hotel DeSoto," he said. "It's one of the oldest hotels in St. Petersburg."

"Okay," I said, putting the paper down.

He looked confused and almost hurt. "Your great-grandfather. You know about him, right? Quincy Monroe? He used to own that hotel. A long time ago, of course."

"What?"

"You know," he said, "the railroad tycoon? Quincy Monroe. They're knocking the place down next week. Luxury mall. Which, by the by, I have a small investment in. Which also, by the by, is only a bus ride from your grandmother's house, no transfers. Another selling point. It's been vacant for years. The old hotel, I mean. It's been tied up in court since, well, since your great-grandfather died. It's coming down now, though. Wanna invest? Ha, just kidding. And no, you don't own any of it. We all checked. Ha."

I stared at the guy. Was he an idiot, or what? That was a lot of random information to just spout out.

"You're saying my great-grandfather owned a hotel?"

He raised his eyebrows high and made a noise in his throat. "Several! And of course Gulf Railroad, for a while. That's what made his fortune." He laid two fat highlighters next to each other, then a third on top, which slipped through and sent the two bottom ones rolling sideways.

"His fortune?" I said. "Dad —"

"Mr. Halbert!" My father snapped. He shook his head quickly, then cut his hand across the air at me. *"Never mind all that,"* he said coldly.

"Dad, wait, a hotel —"

But Randy and Dad shared an intense look. It was the first time the agent's eyes met any of ours. He stopped short and switched gears.

"As I said, I can start showing the house immediately," he went on, staring glumly at our buttons and pushing a sheet of paper across his desk. "Here are a few things you might want to deal with. This list of little repairs might help. Also, keep those windows open. All that dead air, you know. Old people in old houses. Anyway, I don't think we'll keep you in St. Petersburg too long!"

My father just nodded, his eyes dark now, his face tight, as if he were going to cry. Oh, great. That's all I need. What made him go *there*? The old hotel? Selling the house? Realizing that he wouldn't be in his hometown anymore? Telling me that his mother wasn't married? I made as if to get up, and he did, too.

Luckily, he seemed better when we got out on the street again. But I had to chuck it all by asking about the railroad thing.

"Never mind," he said sharply. "It's nothing. That guy doesn't really know what he's talking about."

"Yeah, but . . . hotels? Railroads? Your grandfather? That's big stuff. It's huge."

"Jason, later." He was cold again, dark.

"Sure," I said. "Sorry."

We had a pretty much silent burger lunch, got gas, and drove back to my grandmother's house in that dumb tiny car. He dropped me off while he went out to get supplies. Paint and brushes and nails and stuff, so he could start the repairs before the house was shown.

It's almost bizarre how everything began to happen then.

CHAPTER EIGHT

I had just entered the Florida room to continue packing the buffet, when the phone rang. It was a very loud ring, which made sense since Grandma was probably hard of hearing. I went into the kitchen and answered it.

"Hel —"

"So how smart are you?" said a man's voice abruptly. And loudly. The volume of the call was turned up, too. It was an old voice, raspy and thin and a little muffled. "Because now . . . it's starting."

"Starting? Excuse me? Who is this?"

"Wait, is this the right number?"

I think I laughed. "It's the right number for this house. Do you want to talk to someone here?"

"Well, who's there?" the voice said.

I wasn't stupid. You never tell people that. Still, the man sounded old, so I didn't want to be rude and just hang up. Maybe he really did have the wrong number.

"What number were you dialing?" I asked him.

There was a pause, then a crinkle of paper. "Three, four, four . . . one, nine . . . three, six. What number is this?"

When I realized I didn't even know my grandmother's number, it flashed across my mind that I had never called her. The number on the phone was too faded to read. I looked everywhere.

"Can you hold on a second?" I said.

"Take your time," said the voice.

I set down the phone and found a phone book on the counter. As I checked it, I heard the sound of a siren, beeping, slamming doors, a sound like the clatter of silverware, and a burst of wild cawing, like parrots, in the background of the call, the phone was turned up so loud. Glancing out the window, I saw Mrs. K chattering wildly on a cell phone and laughing.

Man, I hate this place!

Finally, I found my grandmother's name and address in the book: *A. M. Huff, 4028 30th Avenue North.* I took it back to the phone and read the number out loud. "Three-four-four, nineteen, thirty-six."

There was another crinkle of paper and then a laugh. "I was right!"

"I guess so."

"You can learn a lot at a desk."

I frowned. "Uh-huh . . . huh?"

"A desk. It's where you learn stuff," he said. Then, after a pause, he added, "So, how smart are you?"

"What, that again?" I said. "What does that even mean —"

Click. He hung up.

"Fine. Be that way." I slammed the phone down.

I really hate this place!

I stared at the piles and piles of stuff to sort through in every room, but I couldn't stop going over every line of that stupid conversation until I got to the part about the desk.

You can learn a lot at a desk.

Out of the corner of my eye I could see the far end of the Florida room. Just under the windows was Grandma's desk.

I felt a sudden nervous flash in my chest. I moved

toward it, then saw a shape pass by our front window, first one way, then the next, and heard the sound of a motor coming close, then receding.

"What the heck?"

I went out on the front step. The girl who liked to use yard tools as weapons was cutting the grass. She must have taken off her T-shirt because now she was wearing a bathing suit top with her cutoffs.

I don't know exactly what I was looking at or for how long, but she stopped the mower. "Pull your eyes back in your head, Jo-Jo."

I just stared at her. "Uh . . . this is my grandma's lawn . . ."

"No! Am I mowing her yard by mistake? I keep doing that!"

I didn't know what she meant. "No, it's just that this is my grandmother's yard —"

"No kidding, Batman. I've been mowing her lawn for, like, three years? Only I didn't get to it last week because I was away. Dia."

I just looked at her. "Dia?"

"Dia."

"Okay. Isn't that, like, Spanish for *day*?"

"It's a name," she said, staring at my pale face as if I were an unripe fruit or something. At least she wasn't staring at my throat or my ears. "I spell it with letters. Dia Martin. Didn't she ever tell you I've been doing this?"

"I never . . ." I stopped. "No, she didn't. Anyway, Dia. Yeah. Hi."

After using all those words in a row, my tongue must have loosened up or something, because it just kept flapping. "My best friend back home is a guy named Hector. He's Puerto Rican —" That sounded so unbelievably wrong coming out, but my mind darted away somewhere and left my mouth hanging open with nothing else to say. "I mean . . . uh . . . no . . ."

"Hector," she said flatly.

Oh, no, I thought. *Here it comes. You idiot!* "No —"

"And are you going to ask me if I know him because he's Latino?"

"Jeez, no. I mean, why should you —"

She had already started the mower again and was finishing the next stripe of the lawn.

"We're selling the house!" I yelled.

She stopped the mower again, looking amazed that I would speak again. "And . . . what?" she said quietly.

I breathed in. "Sorry, it's just that my dad and I are sell-ing the house. My grandma died yesterday —"

Her eyes widened. "I knew she was in the hospital. She'd been there before. But she always came back. I'm sorry. She was cool. She always smiled at me. Well, at everybody . . ."

"Really?" I said. The girl looked at the ground for a sec-ond, as if she were lost in thought.

"Anyway," I said, "she . . . we're selling the house, so you probably won't have to do this anymore —"

"So fine," she said suddenly, "I won't." She pushed down on the handle so that the front wheels lifted from the grass and steered the mower around.

"Wait. That isn't what I meant." I didn't actually know *what* I meant or why I said anything at all, but I knew we didn't want a half-mowed lawn. "Wait —"

But she flicked her hand up flat without turning and rolled the mower away across the unfinished lawn and down the sidewalk.

What is her problem? Man, I hate this place! I went back into the house, slammed the door, and hunched down on the couch. "Dia? Dia? What kind of name is that, anyway? And so what, anyway?" I heard the mower start up again on some other lawn.

I sat there and sat there. "Where's Dad?" I said out loud. Then I saw the desk again and remembered the phone call.

Stupid phone call! It was crazy to think that just because some nutty old guy said "desk" I'd find something in the desk, or that this was the desk he meant, or that he meant anything at all!

But there it stood, uncluttered and clean, and I hadn't so much as touched it, so I decided to look. The main drawer under the work area was brushed out and empty. All the letter compartments and spaces were empty. The small drawer in the center between the compartments was empty, too. Okay, so Dad had gone through it. He'd done that much in the time before I came. It was only a piece of furniture now.

But when I closed the little drawer, it jammed halfway in, with one side deeper than the other. I tried to jostle it loose, but when I did, something fell into the drawer from above.

It was a postcard.

It must have been taped to the whatever-you-call-the-ceiling above the drawer, but my jerking it around had loosened it. The shiny cellophane tape around its edges was yellow and dry.

The postcard was old. I could tell that when I picked it up because it didn't feel the same as a new postcard. It was heavier, for one thing. When I turned the picture side up, I must have made a strange sound to the empty house.

It was the Hotel DeSoto!

The same hotel the real estate agent told us about! The same hotel my great-grandfather owned!

Holy crow! What is this? Did the caller want me to find this? Did he expect me to find it? What the heck is going on?

I lifted the card to my nose. It smelled dusty and woody, of having been in that cramped desk drawer forever. Maybe for the last, what, fifty years?

Try sixty. The postmark on the back was from San Diego, California, and dated March 4, 1947. There was no message on the card and no name, there was an address typed on it by, it appeared, an old typewriter: *1630 Beach Drive NE, St. Petersburg, FLA.* Was that where Grandma used to live when she was growing up? Dad would know. The address sounded fancy. The card wasn't like any I had seen before. It wasn't a glossy photo of some place with a happy blue sky like modern postcards. What it really looked like was a black-and-white photograph that had been painted afterward. The colors were bright and a little too perfect.

46

Artificial. The green of the grass was as bright as the skin of a lime. The awning reaching out from the hotel was a kind of bright cartoon orange that I thought was meant to be red.

The surface of the card wasn't smooth under my thumbs, either. It had a texture to it, a cross-hatch of lines that gave the picture the feel of fabric, like a painting.

It *was* like a painting, the way the colors were added, but the more I looked, the more I could, I don't know, *feel* what was in the picture. Despite the unreal coloring, it almost seemed as if the fringes of the awning were waving. I imagined the slapping of the canvas pulled tight over its ribbing of pipes. Tables and chairs were set up beneath and on either side of the awning in a courtyard formed by the two jutting wings of the building. They were shaded by a cluster of palm trees in the court. The more I looked at the trees, the more I could hear their sharp leaves clatter in the breeze.

The sixty-year-old breeze.

I closed my eyes and breathed in. The air in the house now smelled of some plant. Eucalyptus from the backyard, I think Dad had told me. I propped the card up on the desk, looked at all the tons of work still to be done in the incredible heat, thought about the lawn mower girl, the strange phone call, thought about Dad and Mom, and got mad.

Hector was in his hammock when I called.

"I hate this place," I told him. "Stupid place. I hate every stupid thing about it!"

"Now don't hold back," he said. "Tell me what you really think."

"First of all, everybody's cracked and weird; second of all, they're insane, even the kids. I actually met one. Probably the only kid in Florida, and she's a total insane-o. Plus it's so hot. It also turns out there's something fishy about my grandma, but I can't tell what it is, except that she was never married when she had my dad, but I'm not even sure I care about that. No, wait. I don't care. Plus, the real estate agent guy is really odd, and I got a cracked phone call from some guy telling me to look in a desk. And I looked in Grandma's old desk and found a hidden old postcard of an old hotel that my old great-grandfather used to own."

"Dude, no husbands, phone calls, hidden postcards. Sounds like a mystery to me," said Hector. "Like in a book."

"It's not a mystery," I said quickly, wondering right

away why I did. "It's nothing. It's just people, cracked people. Plus, all this is happening and it's three hundred degrees. I've been going around soaked all day, especially in my shorts —"

"Dude, enough."

"Well, what a stupid place! I hate it. What's going on there?" I asked. "Tell me everything."

There was a pause, then the sound of a snort. "Oh, all kinds of stuff. Since yesterday, they paved over the school and now there's a racetrack and a pool hall there. Your house, man, your house was turned into a giant aquarium this morning, but it exploded, and now there are sharks everywhere. But nobody cares because they moved Boston to LA and my hammock is on the beach now. Hey, waiter, another piña colada, please —"

"Shut up," I said with a laugh.

"Dude, you have been gone for, like, an hour. Nothing's new."

I realized as we were talking that I had picked up the postcard again and was feeling its texture under my thumb.

"Hey, you know what?" I said. "They call this the 'Sunshine City.' It's the 'Sunshine City' in the 'Sunshine State.' Guess what it's doing right now."

"Raining?"

"No. The sun is shining."

"Imagine," he snorted.

"So, fine. Talk to you in a couple of days. We bury my grandma tomorrow."

"Say 'bye' for me," he said, and we hung up.

CHAPTER NINE

The funeral was set for eleven o'clock the next morning. First of all, I didn't sleep well in the creepy old bed. All night long, I went over the weird real estate agent, then the weird lawn mower girl, then the phone call, and finally the postcard. Why, after all, had it been hidden?

I told Dad about the phone call and showed him the card. He looked at it, said nothing about it, but did tell me that he had gotten a few strange calls himself. It was probably just the same mixed-up guy who couldn't remember the right number.

"Hang up when that happens," he said. "Old people are always making mistakes."

I finally met Mrs. Kee-whatever in the driveway. She was going to the funeral home with us. She seemed like a nice lady, short and round and neat. Her hair was a silver helmet. She wore two hearing aids and glasses, but not thick ones, with a pair of clip-on shades that she lifted into the up position to say hello to me.

"It's a blessing, your grandmother's passing, you know," she said to me, touching my arm. "For everyone."

I smiled at her. "Thanks."

Then I thought, *Blessing? How was Grandma's death a blessing? And for who, exactly?*

She smiled and flicked her shades back down as we got into the Mosquito, she next to my dad and me squashed in the tiny backseat next to a box of clothes.

"So, how long did you know my grandmother?" I asked her. "Did you know her for a long time?"

"What day is this?" she asked.

I looked at my dad in the mirror, and he glanced back.

"Friday," I said.

"Friday," she repeated.

Another look at Dad while she closed her eyes and

tapped on her fingers as if counting. She popped her eyes open and said, "About thirty years, give or take. Heee!" She cackled like a witch on Halloween. "Heee!"

So maybe everyone in this town was "off."

In case my dad couldn't find the funeral home, I had the obituary page in my pocket for the address. But Mrs. K knew where the Brent Funeral Home was, or "Brent's," as she called it. She seemed to know where all the "mortuaries" were, and pointed out a few of them on the way and told us the names of people who had been "laid out" there.

When we got to Brent's, the parking lot was full, which made me scared that I would have to meet all kinds of Grandma's friends. "Everyone," as Mrs. K had said. But the cars were there for another old person. We were shown to a very small room by a narrow pasty-faced man. Except for the coffin, a few flower displays, and about twenty chairs, the room was empty. The place was overcooled, which I thought might have had something to do with it being where they kept the unburied dead.

The coffin was sitting closed on its stand in the front of the room. I liked that it was closed. I had never seen a real dead person before and didn't want to start looking at one. I guess we were there too early. For nearly an hour it was just me, Dad, and Mrs. Kee-something in the front chairs. The room was tiny. The more we sat in it, the tinier it got. At ten-thirty, there was a rush of people from the other service. They jammed the lobby outside the door. They were loud and laughing. A few people looked in, hushed for a second, smiled sadly, then waved or nodded to the three of us. When they drove off in their cars, it was quiet again. It was like that for another fifteen minutes or so.

"They'll come," said Mrs. K, pressing my hand.

"Who? Everyone?"

"They're just so busy," she said.

"Doing what?"

She gave me one of those smiles again, then shared it with the pasty man at the podium rustling papers. He smiled back at her. I couldn't tell if he was just being nice, knew what she meant, had a secret, thought she was "off," or was fascinated by her helmet hair. His name was Chalmers, which seemed oddly right for a funeral director.

Mr. Chalmers.

If he even *was* a director. Maybe he was an assistant director. After all, his name wasn't Brent. And we had the small room. Maybe Grandma's whole funeral was on a budget. That seemed right, too, for my dad. I could just hear Mom complain about how cheesy it was, and him saying nothing, and us all thinking: *loser.*

While Dad went to the bathroom or something, I got up and asked Chalmers about the obituary.

"My dad says that he didn't write this part, about the 'adventurous spirit.'" I showed him the clipping, and the man's face got red.

He frowned, as if not understanding me. "We sometimes have help, you know. Writing obituaries. If we are overloaded."

"Who?" I asked.

"With the deceased, of course," he said, continuing his look. "This is St. Petersburg. They call it —"

"No, I mean, who helped you with my grandmother's obituary?"

Now he seemed offended. He drew back. "Honestly, son, I don't remember. Now, if you'll take your seat, please. The guests are beginning to arrive. We must hurry along."

Hurry? Why?

Gandy Bridge, Six Miles Long, Between Tampa and St. Petersburg, Florida

P-105

CHAPTER TEN

It was about five of eleven when I heard rumbling and *pop-popp*ing outside, like cars backfiring. Or maybe it was a holdup. When the outer doors creaked, there was a rustle of coat hangers — *who wears coats on a day like this?* — and Chalmers began to earn his keep, welcoming an assortment of people into the room.

None of them looked under a hundred fifty years old. The ones who didn't actually roll into the room in wheelchairs staggered to their seats like toys when their batteries run out. The second or third person into the room was a stick figure of a man with a thin white line of mustache, practically no hair, and wearing a slouchy black beret. He slid through the door and took a seat in the back. He looked around so slowly, it seemed if he were filming a movie with cameras in his eyes. He never took off his beret, and his lips moved all the time. It figures that he would be talking to himself. Crazy man. I didn't make eye contact.

At eleven sharp Chalmers eased his way back to the podium, pausing only to open the lid of the casket, which gave me a shudder. Even sitting, I could see the sharp white profile of my grandmother's hollow face above the side of the box. I felt as if someone were sticking icy needles up and down my back.

I turned away to see about ten people in the room now, when the funeral director finally cleared his throat to begin the service. As I turned back, I couldn't help glancing past him to the casket, and I saw more of my grandmother's face than before. Had she moved? Was she trying to get up? Was she trying to . . . *fly*?

No. I'd just shifted up in my chair.

"Thank you all for com —," Chalmers began. He stopped. His eyes were following something moving slowly across the back of the room.

What now?

Turning yet again, I saw a man in a black suit standing behind the back row. Except that he wasn't standing *behind* the back row, he was sitting down in it! I discovered this when he realized that everyone was looking at him, and he actually stood up from his seat. He must have been over six and a half feet tall! His suit, as black and as shiny as oil, was only a bit shorter than a theater curtain. But he was as narrow as a pole, with a little white face on top. He bowed at all the eyes looking at him, then eased backwards out of the room, murmuring: "Excuse please. Sorry. Excuse please."

I almost laughed out loud when I thought of what Hector would think and imagined the look on his face as he said, "Well, he's tall."

But no sooner had the tall man left than a very curvy lady in a low-cut purple suit came in. I mean, what exactly *was* all this? She had a lacy purple veil draped down from her purple hat. It completely hid the lower half of her face, letting only her dark eyes peer through. She sat in the seat left empty by the tall man.

Finally, a round guy about the size of a fourth grader, with reddish skin and a long gray beard streaked with red, sat at the far end of the row that Mr. Beret was in. They shared a cold stare, and the round man murmured, "Zo . . . zo . . . zo . . ."

"Dad, who the heck are these —," I started, but he shushed me as Chalmers cleared his throat once more and finally began to speak.

"Dearly beloved friends of Agnes Monroe Huff . . ."

He went on for a while. It was mostly general talk about souls and spirits and the path of life taking strange turns. Loves and friendships. Health and sickness. Ups and downs. When he said "ups and downs," I remembered what my mom had said about Dad. I wondered what people really meant by it and whether ups and downs were hereditary. What was I having right then? An up or a down?

When I glanced at Mrs. K, she was listening intently, her white face wrinkled up in a white smile.

I wanted to turn and look at the purple lady again, but it would have seemed too noticeable, so I didn't and sat still. I must have zoned out for a little because when I perked up and listened again, Chalmers was going on about the loving soul of someone named Marnie who had merely "flown" through our lives and who still possessed a child's spirit, or possessed a child's spirit again, or was possessed by the spirit of a child or something.

Marnie?

Who was Marnie? This morning's other dead person?

"Oh, dear," Mrs. K whispered, holding my arm. "No, no. That's not right."

I'll say. The others around us took forever to wake up. When they did, I'll bet they were wondering if they were at the wrong funeral, and then, considering the refreshments (which we could hear being prepared on the other side of the wall), if there was any way that they might actually have known this Marnie person.

I turned. "Dad. We should tell him. . . ."

But even as I said that, my father got up from his seat. He went past the podium, ignoring Chalmers, and knelt by the coffin, sobbing into his hands and trembling silently the whole time. I felt embarrassed for a second, then scared. Was this what he had kept to himself all these years? Was he really that broken up about her?

He did this for a long time, while Mrs. K held my hand tightly.

Nobody moved. The place was so quiet, except for the whispering of Chalmers and Dad's whimpering. Finally the crash of silverware for the reception came from behind the wall, and (besides being glad that Dad had arranged for food), I was relieved when everything seemed to reset to normal.

Chalmers rustled a page on the podium and called Grandma "our dear Agnes," and the weirdness with the names was over. My father, however, didn't stop crying.

I glanced around then and saw the lawn mower girl, Dia, sitting by herself a few rows back. I wanted to catch her eye. I was ready with a little smile, but she didn't look away from Dad. She seemed sad, her eyes watery. I realized then that she probably knew my grandmother better than I did. I didn't know her because we didn't talk about her much at home. But was that any excuse? I felt suddenly cold all over, a bad grandson.

"Your father loved his mother so," Mrs. Keese whispered to me.

I was so dense. I hadn't gotten it before. It wasn't a crazy, flying, alligator-battling old lady who was lying dead here. It was his mother. It didn't matter now that she had always been sick. She had died. She'd left him. Left her house. Left the world. And he was sad. His heart was broken. He missed her. He had no father but a made-up one, and he missed his mother.

Bending lower to the casket, he kissed the folded white hands inside it as if he wanted to fall in there after her.

S-58—Oranges Growing at Midway Groves, between Bradenton and Sara...

CHAPTER ELEVEN

Thirty incredibly long minutes later, it was over. The reception I had heard being set up was not for us. In fact, I learned from Chalmers that there was no reception.

"Cold cuts? In a funeral home?" he said, looking puzzled.

"Well, I just thought —"

"Slices of salami, ham, provolone — here?" He waved his hands around. "Olives? Oh, no, no, son."

The jangling forks and spoons I had heard earlier were undertaker instruments, he told me, which freaked me out more than nearly everything that had happened. I imagined sliced legs on silver trays.

I couldn't get outside fast enough. In the sunshine blazing across the white sidewalk, my dazed father and I shook hands with people for about five minutes.

Dia was in line with the others, and I shook her hand. "Listen," I said. "I . . ." I seized up. My fingers gestured in the air as if I was trying to talk with them.

"I'm sorry about your grandmother," she said.

I nodded and was halfway into a swallow when my attention was suddenly taken by a man with a small waist and a large chest, and she walked away. The man hobbled over on bowed legs, saying he was "shorry" for our "losh." As soon as he left, the purple lady with the veil was there, just nodding, answering nothing, saying nothing. She held out a purple glove and shook my father's hand, then mine. Her hand was enormous and her grip weirdly strong. Next to her was the man with the beret and the mustache, who had tiny eyes, one of which rolled slightly outward. He looked at my father, then rolled his eyes to look at me for what I thought was way too long. I tried to smile.

He cleared his throat. "You must be Jason," he said.

"Did you know my grandmother?" I asked in a variation of my conversation starter.

"Coincidentally, yes," he said softly. "Otherwise, it would be odd for me to be here, don't you think?"

That confused me and made me feel a little dumb.

But he went on in a whisper. "Good luck, kid."

"Excuse me —"

"Zat vuz nice, yunk man!" interrupted the barrel-shaped red-and-gray-bearded guy, nudging his way roughly past Mr. Beret. His eyes twinkled as he spoke. I didn't know whether he was talking about what Chalmers had said, the flowers, the casket, or something else. He bowed very low to both me and my father. He clicked his heels, or tried to. When he put his feet together, he wobbled sharply, and the man with the beret grabbed him to keep him from falling. They exchanged frosty looks again and quickly ungrabbed each other. Mr. Beret left in a snit, then the German man nodded with a bright, "Goot day!" He walked the other way down the sidewalk.

My head was aching. Who let the clowns in? Who *were* these people? Friends of Grandma's? Suddenly, the whole *flying* thing didn't sound so strange. *Could I please just be alone for a while?*

I wondered if it was wrong to phone Hector from the funeral home. I needed to laugh.

The whole thing ended with the sound of popping from the parking lot again, which I decided actually was a car backfiring. Soon my father, Mrs. K, and I were on the sidewalk alone with the director, who alternately looked at his watch and squinted down the street.

"Perhaps we should . . . ," he said, motioning to the door.

"Of course," my dad answered, and the two of them went inside to finalize the bill. You have to pay a lot for people to die.

For ancient folks on the tail end of life, everyone who came to the funeral seemed to have somewhere else to be and had to be there right then. I was a little shocked by the way they had all zipped away so quickly, and I told this to Mrs. Keefe.

"Oh, no. It's past eleven-thirty, dear," Mrs. Keese said, her teeth beginning to slip. "Early bird lunch has been going nearly an hour." She made a nod to the end of the street. I squinted into the white air across the white street to a white building with a set of white revolving doors. It was blurry in the haze from the street, but I just made out the last of the funeral guests entering a place called The Driftwood Cafeteria.

Not moving her eyes from the distant doors, she flicked the hinged shades down onto her glasses. "Which reminds me," she said. "I'm getting a little hungry myself. I wonder what today's soup is. . . ."

"But what about the cemetery?" I asked. "Aren't you coming with us? To say good-bye to Grandma?"

She pressed my hand tightly. "Jason, she's not here anymore."

A moment later, she was staggering across the street herself. "Don't wait for me, honey. I'll find a ride home!"

CHAPTER TWELVE

Grandma's house was closer to Bay Pines Cemetery than to Brent's, so Dad decided at the last minute to follow the hearse in his rental car rather than going in Mr. Chalmers' black limousine and having to return to the home.

So there we were: driving the minuscule green Toyota Insect, a black funeral flag suction-cupped to the front fender, behind the thirty-five-foot hearse: a dorky death procession of two.

Still all puffy, my dad was hunched in the seat like a clown at a circus, craning his neck to see out the tiny windshield at the stoplights. He snorted. "Are they seriously going to stop traffic for us? People will cross right in front of us. Why is the hearse driving so fast? Everyone's looking. The police will crack up laughing. Jeez, Jason, we should have taken the black car. This is stupid. It's my mother, after all! Why couldn't I take the other car? Dumb stupid bozo car!"

The *thunk* of dirt on the casket gave me the creeps the way it echoed. The box was nearly empty, after all. There was nothing left of Grandma by the time they'd picked her up from the floor or the couch or the bathroom or wherever it was that she had her stroke. I remembered how thin she was in that photo. I had helped my father and Chalmers and two cemetery men carry the coffin from the hearse to the grave site. She must have been as light as a feather, and I felt so heavy and so tired.

"She's not here anymore," Mrs. K had said.

Hector! Get me out of here!

When we returned to the car, I took one last look at the grave site. A small backhoe was already pushing dirt into the hole. It seemed harsh and cold and final. It was really over now.

"Hecky says bye," I whispered.

Dad and I drove home saying nothing. I couldn't find any words. It smelled of rain, but none came. A few gray clouds passed overhead, the bugs got quieter, the clouds vanished, the bugs got loud again. It was Florida. It was sunny. Which reminded me of something that Randy Halbert had told us. One of the old-time newspapers used to be free for each day the sun didn't come out. They gave away free papers, like, almost never in thirty years.

St. Petersburg was the Sunshine City. The Sunshine City in the Sunshine State. Get used to it.

"Hey, Hector," I said later that night. "It's my daily 'I hate Florida' call."

"So how are you feeling about Florida exactly?"

"I hate it."

"Bold statement. The news here is that all those changes I told you about got reversed. There's nothing happening. It's totally boring. When you coming home?"

"Not soon enough."

"You mean you don't like Florida?"

"I hate it."

My father had had a couple of beers and was nearly asleep. I went to sleep, too. On the couch in the Florida room. After I found out that Grandma had had her stroke in my bed.

CHAPTER THIRTEEN

The Dumpster delivery truck came early Saturday and woke me up with its incredible thudding and banging and clunking. My dad had to run out in his pajamas and repark the Subaru Termite so the guy could leave the Dumpster in the driveway.

There was so much junk! The garage was filled with boxes and bags of I don't even know what and millions of papers and magazines like a library. *Life* magazines and *Time* magazines. When I saw the towering stacks of twined-up newspapers from the last fifteen years, I wondered how many of them Grandma had gotten for free. Dad arranged for a church to pick up some of the big pieces of furniture for a shelter they sponsored, then dragged her old clothes from the closet, searched the pockets, sorted them in piles by type, then folded them (at first, then later just stuffed them) into garbage bags.

Mrs. Keach told him where the Goodwill truck was. He made three trips in the car while I started tossing stuff in the Dumpster that I knew wasn't good enough to sell or donate.

It was afternoon, and Dad was on his last trip when I slumped, exhausted, onto a chair in the living room. The white carton Mrs. K had taken from Grandma's closet sat next to me on the floor. Taped on it was her note in black marker: *Very Important Papers!!!* I wondered what she — or Grandma — would consider very important, so I opened the carton flaps and lifted out a stack of yellow folders filled with old papers. My dad had already gotten the will and the deed to the house from a safe deposit box at the bank, but this was other stuff. Old tax records, home insurance policies, store credits, bills, receipts, manuals for appliances, bank statements, all kinds of records you probably didn't need but couldn't just throw out.

Grandma had signed some of them. On the old ones from the 1960s and '70s, her signature was thin and neat. Later ones were signed more raggedly. On the very recent ones her writing was no more than a scribble. On one, from fewer than ten years ago, there was a scrawl followed by initials ending in K. Mrs. Keesh, maybe? I couldn't tell.

I was just about to leave the carton for Dad to go through when I found something that didn't belong. In a folder marked *EB* was a copy of an old magazine. But it wasn't like *Time* or *Life* or *National Geographic*.

The magazine was called *Bizarre Mysteries* and was dated October 1944. On the cover under the big yellow title was a dark, crazy picture. A man in a suit and tie was crouching, holding a machine gun and firing it. His eyes were staring in terror at something outside the frame of the picture. His jaw was set hard. His suit was ripped, and there was a streak of bright red blood on his arm. It matched the color of his tie. A beautiful woman in a red dress (the same color as the blood and the tie) seemed to be leaping down next to him from a height. Her eyes were filled with fear like his, but a pistol in her hand was blazing with orange flame as she fired at someone or something in the same direction as he was.

But that wasn't the most amazing thing. Behind them a giant alligator lay on its back, its massive jaws hanging open loosely.

Even that wasn't the most startling thing. Behind the alligator were three ghoulish-looking creatures, hardly human, holding long, curved daggers. They wore billowy black capes that shimmered in wild colors like an oily rainbow. They looked like demented clowns, their skull-like heads silhouetted against the dull glow of the background. They were ready to pounce on the man and the woman, who obviously didn't know they were there. To make matters worse, the couple seemed to be in a dismal swamp somewhere, with thick vines and wispy moss hanging down from above. And they were up to their ankles in bubbling black water.

But the most astonishing detail was one I hadn't even caught right away. It was only when I looked and looked did I see that on the woman's back, arching up from her red dress, were what looked like wings — feathery wings of very deep blue, almost invisible against the darkness of the swamp. Wings! A flying lady!

"What the —!" I swore to myself.

Running along the bottom of the cover were the titles

of some of the stories inside the magazine: "Dying the Hard Way," by a guy named Chester H. Dobbs; "Who Killed Owen Taylor?" by Chandler Hawks; "Rock, Paper, Scissors, Gun" by Gerald McHiggins; and "Twin Palms: A Novel of Thrilling Terror," by someone named Emerson Beale.

"Emerson Beale," I said, glancing at the thin letters penned on the folder tab. "EB."

When I heard my father pull up in the driveway next to the Dumpster, I jumped to the door. "Dad, you have got to see this!"

He came into the living room with a bag of groceries and a wad of folded cartons under his arm. "Hmm?"

"Look at this thing," I said.

He dropped the boxes on the couch and set the bag on the kitchen counter. He put a half gallon of milk, more eggs, a six-pack of beer, a loaf of bread, and a bag of sliced cheese in the fridge. Then he pulled out one of the beers and came in and took the magazine. "So what's this? What did you find?"

"Is it weird or what? Grandma kept this in a secret folder in the closet along with regular important papers. Take a look. Skeletons with daggers. Machine guns. Alligators!"

He snorted a laugh. "*Bizarre Mysteries.* Yeah, I guess so."

"But look at the wings! Dad, the wings! Like what Mom said Grandma said. About flying!"

He shook his head quickly. "Yeah, well . . . try to forget all that —" He stopped in the middle of a sip.

"What is it?" I asked.

He held the magazine out and frowned at its cover, lost in thought. "I remember this," he said finally.

"You do?"

"I think so. The colors. And the machine gun detective. And . . . this guy . . ." He tapped his finger at the bottom of the cover. "Emerson Beale. I think she knew him. Your grandma knew him. Yeah, Emerson Beale. She must have said his name when I was growing up. Holy cow, I haven't thought of him in forever. In fact, I think he was her boyfriend." He almost smiled.

"Are you kidding? Grandma had a boyfriend?" Then imagining her old face in the coffin, I began to feel icky, like Mom must have felt when thinking about a flying old lady. An old lady with a boyfriend? And no husband?

"Wait . . . really? A boyfriend? When? Dad, could he have been, you know . . . your . . ."

"Father? No, no, this was when she was young. In high school, I mean. When she was young. He was gone long before I came along. Something happened and . . . did you look through this?"

"I just found it."

We sat in the Florida room and flipped through the magazine together. The pages were old, brown, and brittle. The corners chipped off in our laps as we turned the pages. At the beginning were ads for things like body building ("In just 15 minutes a day, I can make you A NEW MAN!"), jewelry ("GENUINE INDIA-MADE SILVER RINGS"), false teeth for as low as $7.95, how to write and weld and paint and play trumpet and become an accountant and a finger-print expert and how to cure indigestion and asthma at home.

But the stories were the main thing. Some had monsters or ghosts or mummies or doubles or ancient curses, but leafing through them, we could see that they were all dark and dangerous and weird. They were about kidnapping and murder, robbery and murder, robbery and kidnapping and murder, murder and murder, and just plain murder. And they were all written in rugged, tough-guy language.

"Bizarre mysteries is right," I said. "I mean, come on. Alligators and flying women and machine guns?"

He got up and went to the refrigerator. He twisted open a second bottle of beer, moved the important papers carton to the desk, and began looking through the other folders.

"So . . . Dad . . . ," I started.

"Hmm?"

"What's all this about Grandma's father? The railroad thing?"

He shook his head. "It's nothing. It's dumb. He was someone, I guess, but that was so long ago. There hasn't been any fortune forever. He went bust, I think. Broke." Maybe Dad didn't really want to talk about it, but I was just being casual and eventually got him to say a few things, even though he said that nothing meant anything because it was so long ago. Listening to him, I became astonished at the history of my family.

Grandma's grandfather — and my great-great-grand-father — was a guy named Patterson Monroe. Dad said that he was one of the men who brought the railroad to the west coast of Florida in the early 1900s. At that time the state was undeveloped and wild, more like what the Everglades is still — swampy, green, jungly. His son, Quincy Monroe, was Grandma's father. He inherited the big railroad empire from his father and ran it up until the 1960s.

Patterson. Quincy. What names!

"And this guy? Emerson Beale? You really think he was her boyfriend? When she was young?" I said.

"I don't know much," he said. "All I'm remembering is that he wrote cheesy detective mysteries for magazines like this one. But it was when they were really young. Eighteen or twenty or something. He was only around for a little while, then he was gone. Vanished. That was, I don't know, fifteen years before I was born. Longer."

Gone? Vanished? Maybe there actually was a mystery.

"Her father didn't like him for some reason. But then, the old man didn't like anyone." He paused to shake his head. "She talked about him a little, Beale, I remember that. But he went away and who knows?"

I wanted to call Hector right away. Grandma with a boyfriend! From a picture we found earlier in the buffet, I could tell that she was pretty as a teenager. But not long after that she had some kind of accident and didn't get better. She was in a wheelchair most of her life. Dad always said he didn't know what actually had happened to her, only that she nearly drowned. It got very hazy when he talked about it, so I didn't understand much. Maybe Mom was right. It was all pretty strange. But at least he was talking about it.

The Florida room was warming up as the afternoon went on.

Dad finished his second beer and gazed at the floor, not sorting papers, only shaking his head slowly. "It was okay for a while when I was young," he said. "I mean, almost normal. I liked that. I loved growing up here. Who wouldn't? But she was never well, always sick. Hospitals, clinics. I saw her less and less and nurses more. Nannies took care of me for a while. There was money. Then, I don't know, things changed. She was really sick then, and I barely saw her after that. I wanted to stay, but she was vehement that I should go away."

He went quiet and seemed to fall into himself like at home. I totally knew what Mom meant. It was hard to know what to do. Was he going to start crying again?

"Maybe because she was too busy?" I said.

"What?"

"With doctors and all? Maybe that's why she wanted

you to go to Boston? After high school. Because her whole time was spent with being sick and stuff. Maybe?"

He snorted. "Who knows? I hated it. I didn't want to go. I was mad. I wanted to stay in St. Petersburg. I loved it here." He paused. "But after school everyone split up, anyway. My friends went different places. I went to Boston, worked for a while, then went to school. I met your mother there." He paused again. "That was good. Your sister and brother came along, then she got sick. Mom got sick. I mean, my mother, not Mommy, got sick in her mind and nothing was the same. It all . . . it all . . . jeez, Jason, whatever!" He stood up. "Can't you see I don't want to talk about it? Her adventurous spirit has flown — *pfff.*" He made a little sound. "She's dead now, and buried. For Pete's sake. It's over."

He got up and stomped into the kitchen. He grabbed the refrigerator door, yanked it open, and pulled out another beer.

"Just get to work, huh? Leave that box alone; I'll do it. Trash the junk from the buffet, then empty the kitchen cabinets into the boxes I bought. Let's get this moving!"

"Sure, Dad. I'll do it."

I went back to the buffet while he slumped off to the bedroom. I heard drawers slam and clothes hangers jangle, cursing, then it went quiet. A few minutes later, I heard snoring. Well, good. He had, what, three beers in the middle of the day? The sun was pouring into the backyard now; it was deep afternoon. I dragged an empty carton over. I tried for a few minutes to calm down, not sure what to do, until I found myself back at the desk and that magazine in my hands again. It smelled of closets and dust and old things, but also strangely sweet, like chocolate. I sat down and went through it page by page until I found Emerson Beale's story. The story by Grandma's old boyfriend. Taking a long breath to calm myself, I began to read.

CHAPTER FOURTEEN

TWIN PALMS

A NOVEL OF THRILLING TERROR

By Emerson Beale

— I —

THE BLUE SEDAN

There are a hundred different ways to start a story.

For instance, I might begin by telling you about Marnie. Marnie Blaine. Gosh, Marnie!

That stopped me dead. Marnie? *Marnie?* I read the words again and again. Are you kidding? The funeral guy called Grandma that! I'd thought it was just a mistake. Wasn't it? This couldn't just be a coincidence?

"Dad —"

I froze. Dad was still snoring in his bedroom. I couldn't ask him, anyway. He might get angry and have another beer. My heart was pounding. I started to read again.

My heart thumps like a bebop drummer just saying her name. I could begin the story with her. I could end the story with her. Marnie's everything to me.

Maybe I should start with the big old hotel. That's a piece of the story, too, weaving in and out of it all the way to the end. I could tell you about that.

My father? Sure. He may even have started the whole thing, with his simple, "Hey, Nick —"

Or Florida. Crazy old Florida. The way it turns your mind around and makes you see things and feel things and think things that might or might not be there. Florida is as much a part of the story as the hotel is or I am or Marnie is.

I could even start by saying something smart. Like

how everything that happens to me, to you, to everyone, is really part of the same long mystery.

But never mind all that. I'll start with something dumb. I'll start with the blue sedan.

The blue sedan. It's funny how dumb things stick in your head, isn't it? Dumb things and silly things and huge things. They all bobble around inside your brain and get mixed up until you can't tell what's important and what's not.

Like the flash of bullets and a plate of fried eggs.

The glint of a dagger and the color of a guy's socks.

Finally, just when you think your head will explode with everything knocking around inside it, your heart taps you on the shoulder and tells you what's what.

That's how it was the day I finally met Marnie Blaine.

It happened like this.

I was strolling out of a breakfast joint on Third North. It was wartime. I was nearly twenty. But the Army would have to pull up its bootstraps and march along without me. A bum left eye had kept me out of the service and idling on the home front, but I was doing my part with the Florida War Bonds effort.

I was heading for my office, humming a catchy little Cuban dance tune I had heard on the diner's radio, the taste of home fries and eggs still in my mouth, when I heard a funny sound like *chink. Chink.*

I just had time to think, *Funny sound,* when the squeal of tires and the *pop-pop* of a rough engine filled the air. A blue sedan tore around the corner, a series of bright flashes bursting from its side window. Every flash was followed by one of those *chinking* sounds and a spray of brick dust off the wall next to my face.

"Holy smoke!" I shouted to whomever would listen. "I'm being shot at! Hey! Anybody! Help —"

Chink! Chink!

I ducked for safety behind a big green Pontiac just as its driver pulled away from his parking spot.

"It's all yours!" he said brightly, and gave me a wave.

"Thanks a lot, pal!" I yelled, trying to hide behind the thin stalk of a parking meter. I failed.

Chink! Chink! The gunmen were testing their bullets against the sidewalk now. Even as the blue sedan careened toward me, I saw two deep dents on its left fender and a Y-shaped crack on its windscreen.

I remember the dents — dumb things that they were — because even as I scrambled for cover, even in that half second, my mind flashed back to another dented blue car.

The one that had roared past me eleven years earlier.

I was nine.

My father and I were crossing Central Avenue. He was angry, fuming, and panicked about I didn't know what. A car that same color blue had nearly knocked us down in the street. Without thinking twice, we jumped onto the sidewalk, my father sputtering under his breath as the car wheeled by.

"Hey, Nick," he said, "run in there and get us a newspaper. Run into that hotel and pick up a paper."

I looked up at the big place next to us. He said he needed to know about the fight, the big battle in Tallahassee.

"Dad?" I grew scared, because I didn't know about any battle so near us and if people got hurt or how many had died.

"They'll have a paper, Nicky," he told me again, his eyes searching the storefronts from one side of the street to the other. "I'll go to that stand on the corner. But get a copy from the lobby if they have one, will you?"

He gave me a nickel and hurried away along the street, his head stretching every which way, his hands shaking like palm leaves in a storm.

"Okay, Dad, okay." I ran up the steps and stumbled into the lobby. It was the famous Hotel DeSoto. It was vast and rich and fancy....

Whoa, whoa, whoa, *what*? The hotel on the postcard? The hotel my great-grandfather owned? The place being bulldozed next week? No way!

I was sucked in again.

Before I saw anything, before I saw the rack of papers or the neat-haired boy selling them or the long mahogany counter or the silver bell gleaming on top of it or the postcard rack or the gilded columns or the tufted cushions, I saw her.

I saw her. A single willow, all in white except for the pastel green ribbons on each shoulder of her dress and the one in her hair. She was standing in the middle of the carpet, standing like something made of white stone (like a gravestone angel, I thought), except that she was turning to see me, to see what the noise was, startled by my rush into the lobby, and watching me trip past the doorman, nearly landing on my face, her light brown hair waving in the breeze of the doors.

Her green eyes, her hazel-green eyes, were looking at me now and frowning. Those eyes, that white, bright forehead with the hair pulled back from it and tied in that ribbon, were frowning at me, but half smiling, too.

My mouth must have been hanging open, and I froze where I lay, and everything froze.

Who are you? I wondered.

Soon enough a beefy hand broke out of nowhere and snatched hers, shaking loose the scene and starting everything moving again. When my eyes flicked up, I saw a man in a pink suit not quite as big as a circus tent. His fat face was lobster-red; his eyeteeth glistened in his mouth and were longer than any man's I'd ever seen. His dark eyes flashed like pistol shots at midnight. He pulled the girl to him.

Just then my father came into the lobby and right up to me, a paper folded under his arm. He knelt and helped me up from the floor and dusted me off. I remember his hat fell on the floor when he did that.

She spoke then, and I turned away from my father.

"Daddy, is he —," she said.

"Never mind him, Marnie. Let's go," the fat man said.

Marnie!

But he didn't go, not right away. Eyeing my father and me, he reached into his breast pocket and pulled out a silver cigarette case. It had a blue stone in the center of it. He clicked it open, pulled out a cigarette, closed the case, and returned it to his pocket in a flash of silver.

Then he tugged the girl across the lobby to where a group of impossibly thin men in oily black suits held open the door of an elevator. A young man with legs like stilts was loping down the stairs into view. He was far over seven feet, close to eight, a giant-in-training with shoes the size of ash cans. Next to him was a squat balloon, also young, also in oily blacks. A flash of curved silver came from his ample waist, but I turned away. The girl was looking over her shoulder at me, and my mind was filled with her, her hazel eyes, that face, that bouncing waterfall of hair, the shattering of the lobby into pieces like a cracked mirror, the sudden earthquake of her her her.

With that half smile, she drew my nine-year-old heart right out of me. She took it into herself and never gave it back. She has it still. She'll always have it.

"Come on, Nicky," my father murmured as he helped me to the street.

"Do you know that man, Dad?" I asked him. "The large man with the girl?"

He'd say nothing to me then nor for a long time after.

When I found out later that the battle in the state

capital was about land and money, only land and money, I wondered why my father cared so much. When he died two years later, my mother discovered he had nothing. From then on, we were as poor as church mice. Poorer.

But I'll never forget the fat man's eyes. They were as black as swamp water on a moonless night. When my father did speak, he told me about those eyes. He said they were mine shafts of evil. That man, he said, was cold-blooded and a thief who had no soul. He was dead inside. A ghost crawling the earth.

I paused. So what the heck was all this? No soul? And a tall kid at the hotel like the tall man at the funeral? And all at the hotel my great-grandfather owned? I picked up the old postcard. I imagined the lobby inside the front doors. "Okay, this is nuts," I said aloud. "Nutty-nutty-nuts!"

I forgot that Dad was sleeping. He woke up with a start.

"What? Huh?"

I said nothing.

"Jason? Jason!"

"Sorry, Dad," I said, getting up. "It's this story. It's so weird —"

He stumbled noisily out of his bedroom, looked at his watch, and swore. "I've wasted the whole day!"

"Dad, it's only been a half hour —"

"The guy's coming! The real estate agent. You heard him. Why didn't you wake me up?" He put his hands to his temples and clamped his eyes shut.

"Sorry, Dad," I said, closing the magazine. "I'll work."

"I have to fix that gutter in the back. It looks stupid. It makes the whole house look like a dump." He was storming around the kitchen now. "And where is that dumb girl who cuts the grass. Why is the lawn half done? Why would she leave it like that?"

I gulped. "Dad, sorry. That was me. I didn't know. I told her not to —"

He turned to me. "You what? Who are you to tell her anything? What do you think we're doing this for? Have you finished filling those boxes?"

"Dad, let's eat some lunch or something —"

"You haven't done anything! You wasted a whole hour! With that stupid magazine! Give it to me!"

"Dad —"

I wasn't prepared for how quickly he would turn. He flew around and tore the magazine from my hands and threw it across the room. I heard the cover rip. His hand was still moving and knocked Grandma's picture off the buffet. It crashed to the floor and shattered at my feet.

"Dad!" I said, kneeling to the picture.

"Never mind that, do what I told you!" he shouted.

Before I knew it, he was through the kitchen, tugging a hammer and a can of nails from the cabinet under the sink. He swore again and again and slammed out the back door.

Trembling, I watched him toss the hammer to the ground, go to the shed, drag out a ladder, bump it along the ground, and throw it against the corner of the house. He lifted himself up on the first step. Stopping, he turned his head down and looked at me through the screen door. I stepped away. He bent down, picked up the hammer and nails, and started up the ladder again.

I stumbled back to the boxes, shaking, shaking. He had had too much to drink. Mom was right. Never mind. His mother just died. He had no father. He was mad. I got it. Never mind.

When he started banging the hammer on the gutter, I swept up the broken glass and threw it away. Then I picked up the magazine. A three-inch rip across the cover tore one of the wings of the red-dress lady. It hurt to see that tear. I taped it up from behind and began to read again. The hell with him, too, hammering out there. I couldn't help it. Holding the magazine in my hands again, I had to open it. I had to start reading where I'd left off.

All those thoughts flashed in and out of my mind in the time it takes for a bullet to go *chink!*

I slid around the corner and started running down the street. The blue sedan followed. Then I saw the hotel. The same hotel. My feet had taken over, and I was running toward the hotel, my thoughts racing as fast as I was.

Is this why I'm being shot at? Is this what it's all about? The hotel? The girl? Is it about her, after all? Is it all about...Marnie?

I raced down a cut-through between two halves of a block while my mind, my silly mind, tried to put the pieces together and flew back again, this time to that very morning, exactly one hour before....

It was only seven-thirty, but already the air was as heavy as wet wool. My shirt was clinging to me like a new bride. I was just imagining a plate of hot eggs in a cool diner and thinking I'd unstick myself from that street bench I seemed glued to, when there she was again.

Sure, it was eleven years later, but I had never forgotten the girl from the hotel. How could I? Now she wore a dress the color of pale butter. But when she looked over, I was the one who melted. She saw me, shimmered slowly up to the bench, and smiled.

"I've seen you before," she said, light flickering in her eyes.

I stood up, remembering the lobby and her, and my tongue started moving. "You remember eleven years ago? In the big hotel on Central?"

She smiled that same half smile as the first time, tinged now with something like a blush. "Sorry, no. But I do remember a few months ago. You were running like you needed to catch a train. Only there wasn't any train. It was at Mirror Lake. You were jumping down the library steps, holding a stack of paper like a serving tray."

I laughed. "Deadline. I'm a writer."

"What's your name?" she asked.

"Falcon," I said. "Nick Falcon. Yours?"

"Marnie Blaine."

"Blaine?" It came to me. "The fat man —"

"My father, Quentin Blaine," she said. "He owns that hotel, I suppose. And the Gulf Railroad."

"But only about half of Florida," I said.

She kept smiling. "Some greyhounds, a hideous new

autogyro, and a racehorse or twenty. But really. No more than that."

Behind her, a man was doing a pretty poor job of pretending to be invisible. He was so much taller than the palmetto he was standing behind that the upper branches might have tickled his chin. The guy was as tall as a house and as lanky as a stovepipe. If he was Mutt, Jeff stood next to him: a little round barrel with a red beard. Too bad there was no fireplug for him to hide behind; he might have had a chance. I'd seen them both before at the hotel when I was nine, only they'd grown. One up, the other sideways.

The giant's face showed no anger or menace. In fact, there didn't seem much life in it at all. I thought again of what my father had told me about faces like that. Was he someone else without a soul?

"Maybe this is too risky," I said, looking at the goons. "Maybe I should send you a postcard."

I nearly choked. A . . . *postcard?!*

She laughed. "A postcard. That's slightly nuts. What for?"

"With a clue to show you where we can meet. A clue delivered all safe and sound by the U.S. Post Office. I write mysteries, remember?"

She smiled. "I'll have to read one someday."

"You'll be in one," I said. "I'll write a story just for you, Marnie Blaine."

The tall man drifted back into the shadows, satisfied to have seen whatever he was looking for. Redbeard rolled quietly after him. I didn't like the look of that. Two ghoulish guys making snap judgments, then running off to tell their boss. It was the scenario for a cheap story, and I knew it; I'd written a few of them myself.

"Never mind the postcard," I said. "The Pier."

"Daddy keeps his autogyro at the Pier. But you don't want a ride in it. He's just learning to drive it."

"No thanks," I said. "I leave flying for the birds. And for angels. Like you." I imagined her at that moment with a pair of bright wings, rose and white and shimmering blue. I liked what I imagined, and it must have shown on my face, because her eyes twinkled.

"I really should be going," she said. Only she didn't move.

"The Pier. For lunch," I said. "And try to ditch the undead."

"They're always around. My father likes to know who I talk to."

"Funny," I said. "I don't care who *he* talks to. Meet me?"

"Maybe I won't be able to," she said.

I smiled at her. "Yeah, you will."

That put a smile on her lips. She walked away then. I followed at a distance and saw her get into a car. It was a cream yellow Phaeton and beautiful. It didn't have any dents. Its windscreen was the opposite of a cracked one. The thing gleamed like a Roman chariot on race day.

I must have stood there frozen like a garden ornament with a dopey grin, because the driver, a wobbly pole of a guy with a skull for a face, saw me, came over, grasped my arm with fingers of bone, and asked me if I wasn't forgetting my appointment. When I said I didn't have an appointment, he offered to make me one with a doctor. I took the hint and hit the bricks.

My stomach told me I needed some eggs.

My heart told me I needed to see her again. I can't explain it. *How could I not want to see Marnie again?*

So there I was, dashing down the alley to the sidewalk, and there were the bullets again, going *chink-chink-chink* at my heels, and all I was thinking about was her.

I nearly made it to the far corner when a shot grazed my calf, and I went down like an arcade target at a state fair. The sedan screeched to a stop a full half inch from my head.

I tried to squirm away into a flower shop, but Redbeard and Mr. Tall weren't having any. They burst from the car and tackled me before I got to the door.

"Just — a — carnation —" I winced.

The tall man clamped his hammy hand on my mouth. Together, he and the barrel pulled me to my feet, dusted me off, and tried to interest me in a quaint little alley they had in mind.

"You're real estate agents?" I grunted. "And I could have sworn you were punks."

That didn't crack half a smile between them.

"Alley," the tall one breathed. "Now."

I said, "I would, but I'm late for my shuffleboard date —" I tried to hobble away, but they were persistent and dragged me into that alley, anyway.

"You're a credit to your boss," I said. "By the way, just to be clear, is your boss a fat guy the color of cooked lobster —"

I doubled over when the giant punched me in the gut. His fist was only as big as a battering ram.

To make a long story short, I never did meet Marnie at the Pier, but I did get a chance to ride in that dented blue sedan. It wasn't the kind of ride they advertise on the radio, all picnic baskets and yodeling kids. The car backed into the alley with us. Skullface swung out of the driver's seat and sauntered to the back of the car. His oily suit swished in the shadows.

"I tell simple words for you, boy," he said, as if he had learned how to speak from a book, or a robot, or maybe a book written by a robot. "She there, you not there. She here, you not here. She everywhere, you nowhere. Good. Now I think you understand it, eh?"

"I think I got it," I said. "Can I go see her now?"

I fell to my knees when he kicked my wounded leg. He kicked me so many times, I couldn't help noticing that he was wearing yellow socks with little blue anchors all over them. Stylish. I was about to ask him where he shopped when the bearded German grunted, "Enuf. Not here!"

"We're gonna take you to da post office," said the giant.

Post Office? Had they read my stories?

"Ya!" chuckled Redbeard. "Vee goink to *post* you!"

"To where," I managed to say.

"Everywhere!" said the giant with a laugh.

"You guys been reading Spinoza?" I asked.

I got a final glimpse of yellow sock near my nose before Mr. Skull straightened his suit — all that kicking had rumpled it. He drew a set of car keys out of his pocket, unlocked the trunk, and held it open while the other two goons scooped me up off the ground and poured me inside.

There was something rotten in there that had attracted a few million flies. They were soon done with it, though. I was fresh meat to them.

Just before they slammed down the trunk lid, I heard one of the thugs say, "Gandy."

Turns out the real estate men knew something about architecture, too. We were going to Gandy Bridge. I guessed their "post office" was an underwater branch, and the posts they were talking about were the concrete ones that supported the bridge. They were going to tie me to one and hope that the fish and maybe an alligator or three would eliminate the evidence.

We drove off at high speed. In the dark of the trunk, I imagined the turns between downtown and the bridge. I remembered that feeling of sand under the tires just before you hit the bridge. The sedan would have to slow a bit or shimmy on the highway. It would be my last chance to escape before they pulled off the road and carried me down beyond the scrubby palms and sand to where the posts were. There wasn't much time.

My legs were like stalks of pain. My eyes burned. My lungs felt like lead. My nose was filled with the stink of something dead, and I wondered if I was smelling my own future. I decided not to dwell on it. I slipped off my belt and started working on the lock with the prong of the buckle. The sedan tore through the streets, fast, fast. After a while, we jerked right; then I felt the tires tearing over sand. They slowed. Then —*click*— the lock opened.

"Timing!" I whispered. Edging the trunk up, I jumped out, hit the ground, and rolled clear just as the car picked up speed again and bounced off into the shadowy undergrowth.

I looped my belt back on and took off as fast as my sore legs could carry me. With my wounded calf, it wasn't all that fast, but for the moment I was alive and free. How long I would be either was anyone's guess.

End of Chapter I

S.83—Alligators in Tropical Florida
Sarasota Jungle Gardens

CHAPTER FIFTEEN

I was quaking all over, barely able to breathe. Grandma's boyfriend had written this story. A guy named Nick Falcon met a girl named Marnie in my great-grandfather's hotel. The funeral guy had called Grandma "Marnie." I saw the posts under the Gandy Bridge. I saw the tall man and the short German. Was this a story based on things that really happened? Would Dad know?

Would he tell me?

I wondered, of course, whether Emerson Beale could be Dad's father. He was Grandma's boyfriend, after all. But Dad said Beale went away long before he was born. I wanted to read the story again — every word — but before I could turn back to the beginning, I saw a small box outlined in black at the bottom of the last page.

A Note from the Editors

Chapter II of "Twin Palms" would have appeared in the next issue of *Bizarre Mysteries*. It is our sad duty to report that Emerson Beale was killed in action on the island of Saipan in June of this year. His passing will be mourned. It is to his memory that we dedicate his unfinished story.

I stared at the black box. My heart thudded, then skipped. My throat was thick. I couldn't swallow.

He died? Emerson Beale died? *His passing will be mourned?*

I felt as if I had been kicked in the chest. Whatever thoughts I had about who Dad's father might have been couldn't include Emerson Beale anymore. He died in the war almost twenty years before Dad was born.

But even more amazing was what I found written in the margin of the last page. In thin blue ink, in neater penmanship than I have ever seen, were words in what I knew was my grandmother's handwriting:

your Marnie forever

So that pretty much confirmed it. Grandma was Marnie. If Emerson Beale was Nick Falcon, he had been good to his word. He had written a story for her. Only it was a story with no ending.

I took up the postcard again and began to study it. Could there have been a clue on it, as Nick said in the story? Was that what the caller wanted me to find? I turned the card over and stopped short. I read the postmark again.

1947.

Emerson Beale died in 1944.

I stood up and paced the room. "The card couldn't have been from him," I said to myself. "He had been dead for three years before it was sent. So who sent it? And why was it hidden that way in the desk —"

I heard the sharp sound of scraping metal outside the back door and then a yell.

"No —!" my father cried. "Oh, Gawww —"

I jumped into the kitchen in time to see the ladder slide down across the back of the house followed by a deep *thump*.

"Dad!" I cried, rushing out the back door.

The ladder was lying across the bushes. My father had fallen off the house and hit his head on the concrete patio.

"Dad!" I said. "Dad!" He was doubled in half and not moving. "Dad!"

4A-H806

CHAPTER SIXTEEN

For what seemed like hours, he didn't move. Then he blinked his eyes and swore. "Holy —!" I was never so happy to hear him curse. "Dad, are you okay?"

He swore again. "No . . . oh, man . . . Jason . . ." He let his head settle back onto the patio, moaning and clutching the side of his face. One of his ears was bleeding from the inside.

"It's okay. Don't move so much."

Mrs. K's door opened, and she came out, her arms full of wet laundry. She was humming. When she saw us on the ground, she screamed.

"Call 9-1-1!" I said. She turned this way and that, then finally dropped the wet clothes on her stoop and scurried inside.

Dad rolled over the corner of the patio onto the grass, clutching his head until he went still, blinking his eyes at the weird angle of his left leg. It was bent in a way that looked like a cartoon character might be able to snap it back into place, but not a person. He looked for a while at his leg, groaned weirdly, then sank bank.

"Oh, gawww . . . oh, jeez . . . Jason . . ."

"Don't try to talk," I said. "An ambulance is coming."

"I called them!" said Mrs. K, stepping through the side yard. "A few minutes is all —"

She was right. It wasn't long before I heard the siren and again not long before the ambulance screeched into the driveway. Two women rushed around to the back with a couple of packs. They twisted Dad carefully into a more or less normal shape, him yelling with each small movement, then lifted him onto a collapsible gurney a man brought around. They strapped Dad's head tightly with braces and Velcro straps. Mrs. K was clutching my arm the whole way around the side yard to the van.

"St. Pete General," said a medic, and one of the women

hopped behind the wheel. A police car drove up now. An officer jumped out and helped the others slide the gurney into the van.

"You're going, too?" the policeman asked me. Before I could answer, he asked, "Where's your mother? Is she here?"

"In Boston," I said.

"What? Boston?" he said, slipping the radio from his belt.

"Get in!" said the man in the back of the van.

"I'll meet you at the hospital," said Mrs. K.

My legs took over, and I headed for the van. Before I got in, I glanced back at the front door of the house.

"Never mind that!" said Mrs. K. "I'll lock up the house. I have a key —"

"Grab your father's wallet first," shouted the officer, running to his car.

The next hour was a blur of streets and sirens, then doctors and nurses and slamming doors and ramps and running through hallways, until it all stopped and a doctor met me outside the emergency room and told me Dad had a concussion, bruises on his shoulders, and his shin bone was fractured.

"He was drinking, I guess?" the doctor said. "And he fell off the ladder onto a concrete patio?"

I tried to take it all in. I nodded. "He had a little, I think."

"More than a little," he said, glancing at his clipboard. "He'll be here for a few days. Is Mrs. Huff around?"

I looked blankly at him, thinking for a second he was talking about my grandmother.

"Your mother?" he said. "Is she here?"

My mother never called herself Huff. She had kept her maiden name. She was Jennifer Gampel.

"No," I answered.

"Your dad is awake now. For a little while. When will she be coming? Soon? Did you call her? Do you want us to call her?"

"No, I mean, she's not in Florida," I said, suddenly worrying if this was a problem.

The officer came in then and came over to us, and the doctor said, "We might have to call Family Services."

Family Services. It actually sounded like something we could use.

"No, no," I said. "I'm just down here with my father from Boston for a little bit. My grandmother just died."

"All right, look. Your father's going to be here for three, four days at least before he can come home. I'd like you to call your mother," said the doctor. "Come over here." He was kind of snippy, as if he had more important things to do. He stepped to the emergency counter, where the desk phones were. The officer followed us. It was all going so fast, but the moment I looked at the phone it flashed through my mind what would happen when I called.

Mom would just pull me out of here. Even if she cared about Dad, she'd be so mad, she'd yank me straight back to Boston, leaving him in the hospital. Then he'd slink back when he got better, and the silences and icy comments would quickly explode into a final argument, and we'd split up completely.

I hated this place, this stupid heat, the smells, and all these nutty old people and dead bodies, but I couldn't forget the way Dad was at the funeral. He was sad. He was miserable and sad and had too much to drink and hurt himself. So okay. He wasn't drunk all the time. And the yelling and breaking stuff? Okay, I was stunned, but I got it. He wasn't a psycho. He'd never done that kind of thing before. His mother just died.

Besides, I could probably stay with Mrs. K, right? Of course. She'd want me to. She would be there soon. I was hoping she would be enough for them, the police. She seemed nice, if a little cracked. I could stay with her.

But Mom? Maybe if things got worse, a lot worse, I'd tell her what happened. But now? No. If she came now, she'd mess it up. She'd push and push then bring me home. And why? So she could leave on another trip?

No, keep it simple. Say nothing. Talk to Dad first about everything. It was only a few days!

All this flashed though my mind in a few seconds, and I knew right then that I was about to do something really serious, but that I was going to do it, anyway. "I'll call her right now," I said, glancing at my watch. "She's at work." I put my hand into my pocket and, making as small movements as I could, I turned off my cell phone.

Why was I doing this? They'd know, right? They'd know.

The nurse at the desk smiled and slid a phone toward me as she handed me back my dad's wallet and a plastic bag of his stuff. "Sure. Dial nine, then the area code. Here." She pressed a button on the phone.

The doctor and the officer were looking at me, talking, and doing a lot of head wagging. I tapped in the number slowly then turned away. The phone rang on the other end.

"Uh . . . hi," I said.

"Dude! Is it raining yet?"

"Look, Hector, I'm in the ER with my dad," I said quietly. "He fell off a ladder."

"What the heck?"

"I know, but everything's okay for now. And he'll be out of here before you know it. Look, they think I'm calling my mom, but I can't do that yet. But don't tell anybody. Not your mom. And definitely not my mom."

"How about nobody's mom?" he asked.

"Perfect."

"Heck, dude, the ER. I hope he's okay. But look, especially be careful to make no eye contact there. I mean it. The patients are, like, halfway across."

"I know, but it's okay for now. I gotta go."

Mrs. Keefe was standing in the waiting area when I got off the phone, and I asked her if I could stay with her for the next few days.

"Of course, dear. I've already talked with the officer," she said. "I have ice cream and plenty of tuna fish."

The doctor saw us talking, then shared a look with the police officer. They both gave me a look. I told them that my mother would call back a little later; she was at the airport for another flight, but would get here as soon as she could. Until then, I'd be at Mrs. K's house.

The officer relaxed. "Okay. Could I have your mother's cell number?"

"You can't call her now because she'll be in the air," I said.

"Fine, but for later," he said.

Gosh, what a little creep I was. I told him her cell number with the last two digits reversed. He jotted it down. He likely wouldn't use it for a while at least. By then, I'd be back at the house, and things could have changed, anyway. I could always say I got the numbers mixed up because I was upset about my dad getting hurt.

"Okay," he said.

I tried not to lie, really. It was more like bending the truth. To say something that wasn't exactly a lie, but wasn't the whole truth, either; that was hard. But I felt I had to give Dad a chance here. Mom was waiting for him to drink too much and to mess up, and he had done both. But it wasn't so bad, was it? It wasn't as if he had had a car accident. He had only hurt himself. And it was just for a few days. We could get past this.

"You can go in now," said the doctor, and he turned and walked briskly down the hall.

CHAPTER SEVENTEEN

The emergency room was a small area with a medical station in the middle surrounded by three walls of open cubicles. Curtains separated the beds from one another. A woman in scrubs pointed me to the farthest one. "Pull the curtain back. He's not asleep."

I peeked into the space. My knees buckled when I saw Dad. His head was bandaged on one side down to his chin. His left eye was swollen and dark. One leg was outside the blanket, propped up and bandaged. Cables dangled from his bed, attaching his finger and his chest to two different boxes, and tubes hung from a couple of bags behind his head. He had an IV pack dripping from a post on wheels.

Holy crow, I thought. *Maybe I* should *call Mom.*

"Dad . . . ?" I whispered. "Dad . . ."

He opened his one good eye and rolled it over to me. Without moving his head from the pillow, he said, "I'll finish the gutter when I'm out."

I nearly spurted a laugh. "Jeez, Dad! Are you serious? Forget the stupid gutter! How do you feel?"

"Don't you do it," he said.

"Right. I'm going to run straight up that ladder. Of course, not. Forget the gutter. I'm sure the real estate guy will understand if not everything's done."

He breathed in with a raspy, wet sound. "Call him, will you? His card's on the kitchen counter. Put off the showings for few days. Until Monday at least. Nothing this weekend. And ask that girl, Diane or whatever, to finish the lawn. Tell her you made a mistake, and you want it cut. And call," he said, his voice a hoarse whisper now, "call your mother, too. Tell her to come down. You can't be in that house alone."

I swallowed, tried to swallow, still shaking. "Mrs. Keese-Keefe arranged with the police that I could stay with her for a few days. She can watch out for me. Or I can watch out for her. Whichever," I said, trying to be funny but sounding lame.

"Good. That's good. But call Mom."

"Dad, do you really want her here —"

"Jason, just do it!" he snapped. Then he turned sullen, as if he knew what would happen when she came. Did he *want* her to take me back? His forehead creased up in pain, and he lowered his eyes. Eventually, his face relaxed. "Jason, look . . ." There was a long pause. "I've been stupid, really, really stupid. I drank too much. I'm sorry. . . ."

My throat was letting almost nothing through. "Dad, it's okay. Don't . . . you know. Don't worry about it."

"I'm sorry I . . . exploded," he said.

"I know."

"Gosh, Jason, I . . ." he flicked his eyes closed, then open. "I love you. I'm sorry. It's just that . . . without her, and closing up the house, and everything, I feel so . . ."

He was starting to cry now and didn't finish. It was a quiet sort of crying, like at the funeral.

"Dad —"

He slurped in his runny nose. "You know we're on

pretty rocky ground, your mother and me. You know that, right?"

I nodded. "Yeah. I know."

"It wasn't always like that. . . ."

"I know."

His face twisted in pain again. "You have nothing to do with it, you know that, too, right?" He stopped. His face cleared. "I'm really sorry. I didn't mean to get so mad, Jason. I'm such a jerk. I'm sorry."

"Dad, it's okay."

We were quiet for a while. His eyes were closed. He didn't move. I thought he was asleep, then he said, more quietly still, "Jason, call your mom. This isn't good. She needs to come."

I could already hear her. "Oh, my gosh, Jason! Your father's in the hospital? Was he drinking? He was drinking, wasn't he? I'm coming as soon as I can. I'm taking you home!"

"Jason —," he said.

No, I thought. No way. You're sorry. Your mother died. You won't do this again. You won't get stupid drunk. You're not such a loser. You're not.

I think things changed in some little way at that moment. Not calling Mom when the doctor and the policeman asked me to was one thing. But knowing I wouldn't
call now that Dad had asked me to made me feel different.
Maybe I felt pushed around by the way they didn't get
along. I had to be quiet at the dinner table. I had to pretend
everything was okay. I had to go to Florida. I had to pack
boxes. I had to call Mom.

Now it was different. Dad was in that bed and Mom
was away and I was on my own for a little while, for a few
days, anyway.

No. I wasn't going to call her. Not yet. Not right now.
It was okay this way. I was okay.

Minutes later he actually did drift off to sleep, and a
nurse said they would monitor his vitals closely for the
rest of the day. Good. He needed to be out of it for a while.
To not think about stuff. Good.

Mrs. K was waiting in the hall. She took my hand as
soon as she saw me. "Jason, how is he?" I told her what the
doctor had said. Then she asked, "Did your mother call
back yet? Would you like me to call her?"

"No, she'll call me," I said, almost believing it myself.

"She's working on a plane connection now. She said she'd get back to me in . . ." I made a move to look at my watch and pretended to calculate. "An hour and twenty minutes."

The "and twenty minutes" came to me as an after-thought. I felt the more accurate I could make it, the more it sounded as if I were really expecting Mom to call.

Mrs. Keefe relaxed. "Good boy. Ask her how her day was."

When I got outside the ER and into the hot air without running into either the doctor or the policeman, I felt free. The sticky air actually felt good. I had a few days more or less to myself.

We were back in Grandma's house in ten minutes or so, but it was another hour before Mrs. Keese finally stood up from the couch and went to the door.

"Well," she said, "quite a morning, wasn't it? Let's have tuna fish sandwiches, all right?"

"Sounds great," I said. "But maybe later. For supper?"

"Three-thirty?"

I swallowed hard. "I want to do a little packing before it gets dark. I was thinking more like . . . five o'clock?"

"Ooh, late!" she squeaked. "All right, Jason. Five

o'clock, then. I'll make up the extra bed. Call if you need anything. Anything at all."

Her steps clacked away down the concrete walk. When I heard the *slunk-slunk* of her shoes on the cement steps leading to her door, the squeak of the screen, then nothing, I knew I was finally alone. At last. It was just after one o'clock. For four hours I'd be alone. Then dinner, then maybe alone again.

This was great. I needed to get my head back. I needed to be quiet. I needed to be alone.

Gandy Bridge, Six Miles Long, Between Tampa and St. Petersburg, Florida

P-106

CHAPTER EIGHTEEN

I dumped myself onto the couch in the Florida room and just breathed in slowly for about five minutes. Maybe I dozed off. Maybe I just sat there. I don't remember. But soon my eyes were open and staring at the magazine and the postcard on the desk.

Bizarre Mysteries. The Hotel DeSoto.

I sat down and read Emerson Beale's story again. And a third time. Every word. The pages were rough to the touch, old and ragged along the edges. The heat of the house made the pages smell even sweeter than before. The more

I read, the more I could hear his voice speaking quietly in the room, as if he were talking only to me.

`I might begin by telling you about Marnie.`

But each time I read the story again, I came up against that line in the box at the end.

It is our sad duty to report that Emerson Beale was killed. . . .

It hurt to read that, something in me ached over those words. He died, and the story was unfinished. How did it end? Okay, it was just a story. It was made up. A magazine story that maybe had something to do with Grandma, or maybe not. No, probably not. Not really. It couldn't. But not to have finished writing it? To be just . . . *dead*?

Grandma was dead now, too. I wondered how she had felt when she read the words in that black box. That was a question, wasn't it? How *she* felt? If Emerson Beale was someone she loved, and if they met even a little like that — she did call herself Marnie, after all — how did she feel?

My hands trembled when I picked up the postcard. Did

it contain a clue like the story said? If the card were hidden as it seemed to have been, maybe there actually *was* a clue.

I must have turned the card over and over a dozen times and ran my fingers over it, turning it this way and that and reading every word on it before I saw that in the phrase describing the hotel, ". . . spacious lobby, air conditioning in every room, veranda, patio . . ." the words *air conditioning* had two tiny dots under them. The dots were so small and so faint, they might not have been anything other than accidental marks. So okay, it might have been nothing after all.

Then I found something else.

In the message area, nearly invisible to the eye, were two short parallel lines pressed into the message area as if by a typewriter without a ribbon. The lines were crossed like T's on the top and also on the bottom. When I realized that what they really formed was this —

II

— it was like a hammer struck me on the head. *Are you kidding me!* I turned to the note at the end of the story and read that line again:

Chapter II of "Twin Palms" would have appeared . . .

Chapter II. II! But *what* about Chapter II? Did the post-card mean that Chapter II was *about* the hotel? Was the hotel where something *happened*? Was Chapter II *hidden* in the hotel —

Wait. Emerson Beale died in 1944. This card was sent in 1947, three years later. It wasn't possible. How was it possible? Who sent the card? What gives?

At that moment, nothing gave. But my thoughts flew around and around the whole thing until it was five o'clock and the phone rang, and Mrs. K chirped into the phone, "Tuna sandwiches!"

We ate a supper in which I must have said, like, nine words to the lady, while she rattled on about taxes and trash pickups and bus stops, then quieted and said that I probably wasn't talking much because I was sad about my grandmother and worried about my father but that we'd visit him in the morning.

"Thanks," I said. "Some day we had, huh?"

"Oh, yes, dear. Yes, we had."

"I'll be back tonight at eight or so," I said. "I'd really like to do more packing for when Dad gets out. Is that okay?"

"What a good son," she said.

It wasn't quite six when I got back to Grandma's house.

My cell rang while I was still on my own doorstep. It was Hector.

"How's your dad?" he asked.

"All right, I guess. He'll be in the hospital a few days, in a regular room. He looked bad, but he was sleeping when I left him."

"I was doing that today," he said. "Sleeping. In my hammock."

I told him about the ultra-strange funeral guests, that I saw the lawn mower girl at Brent's, the story, the phone call, the postcard, and the dead boyfriend. He said I had told him about some of those things before. I guess I wanted to get the whole thing out in the air again, where I could hear it. It didn't help much. None of the pieces connected or made sense.

"So, you still hating the place?"

"More than ever," I said.

"That's my boy."

"There are hummingbirds in my backyard," I said.

"In your backyard?" he said. "Cool. They're really tiny, aren't they? You can't see their wings except in pictures. I read that once. Somewhere."

Entering the Florida room, I looked down at the cover

of the magazine and really wanted to get off the phone. "Call you tomorrow," I told him.

"The Hammock King awaits, O voyager!"

With all those empty boxes to fill and all that work around the house, the packing, the cleaning, it was only a matter of time before I was into the magazine again.

I started at the first page and tried to read the other stories, but kept drifting back to Marnie and the blue sedan. But it always ended without ending.

For the moment I was alive and free. How long I would be either was anyone's guess.

It was almost as if he knew.

I put away the ladder, hammer, and nails, and sat in the backyard for a long while. The sun was nearly down, but it was still hot. I was sticky in my shirt. A swarm of tiny bugs hovered in the fading sunlight. Their high-pitched whine was the loudest thing except for two men a street or two over pounding, moving boards, pounding, yelling loudly, pounding again. They'd have to stop soon, I thought. Darkness would stop them. It would be night.

I went back in the house, put the magazine, the postcard, my pajamas, and toothpaste in my backpack, grabbed my pillow, locked up, and walked over to Mrs. K's house. As I was crossing the yard, I saw Dia and (I guessed) her mother on the sidewalk. They turned to look at me. I was suddenly embarrassed to be seen carrying my pillow as if for a sleepover. Whatever.

The room Mrs. Keene had made for me was small and neat. The light on the nightstand was already lit when we said our good-nights and she left for her own room. The walls were decorated with framed photographs, old black-and-white ones and more recent ones of colorful flowers and birds. I took out the magazine and set it on the nightstand and propped the postcard against the base of the lamp.

My mind was a jumble of questions.

I wanted to ask Dad what was going on. Did he even know? Why did he have to drink so much, anyway? And why was Mom so cold? I mean, she wants to understand, but she doesn't. How am I supposed to? This postcard didn't have anything to do with anything, did it? Why would Grandma hide a postcard of the Hotel DeSoto, which her father supposedly owned? And this story? Was any of it true? Was Grandma really Marnie? You cried at the hospital and before at the funeral, Dad. Are we splitting up this summer? Is Grandma's funeral just a convenient way for that to happen? Is that why I'm down here? Am I an up or a down?

I could hear him answering with an edge in his voice, "Dump all that junk, will you? Get to work. I don't know what the postcard is about. I don't know about your mother. Or my mother. Or my father. I don't know about Emerson Beale or Grandma or Nick Falcon or Marnie. I don't know about the story. I don't know anything about anything. Dumb stupid bozo car!"

The darkening room closed in on me. It remained hot.

Except that maybe Dad wouldn't yell this time.

Maybe it was different now. Wouldn't anyone go off the deep end who was close to someone and she died? And you could never talk about her because she was nutty, but now you had to clean up her stuff and sell her house and shut it all down and that part of your life was over?

I got up and slid the window up. The air was warm, but fresher. I sank back down again. Tiny bugs whirred and spiraled in the lamplight, all of them making an *eeeee* sound, as if heat had a sound and the bugs were making it and they knew it and they liked making it. I watched them and watched them, leaning on my elbow, until I saw something else happening.

CHAPTER NINETEEN

Staring down at the magazine on the nightstand, I realized that the eyes of one of the menacing dagger men were glowing. Glowing! That part of the picture was nearly black in the rectangular shadow of the postcard, but his eyes shone in a very tiny, but perfectly round spotlight. I moved my hand over the magazine, and the spot of light played across my fingers. I knew what some part of my brain had already guessed: that the light wasn't actually coming from the attacker's eyes.

But where it actually *was* coming from was odd enough.

It was coming — I knew because I followed the tiny beam back up with my fingers — it was coming from the postcard.

The moment I moved the card, the light disappeared. But when I held it up to the lamp, there it was again, a tiny twinkling light. There was a hole in the card, a puncture so small and yet so perfectly round, it looked as if it had been put there on purpose with the tip of a needle.

My heart fluttered. The hole had been been poked through the window of one of the upstairs rooms of the hotel, as if that room were important. As if something might be found there. My hands trembling, I turned the card over and studied the II pressed into the message area, and the words *air conditioning* with the dots under them in the description. Were these clues? To some kind of mystery?

I could hear Hector say, "Mystery? You said yourself there's no mystery, just wacky people. Dude, the heat is *so* getting to you."

Maybe it meant something. Maybe not. Maybe the postcard contained a clue. Maybe it was random. Maybe "Twin Palms" was just a cheesy story with no ending.

Maybe the boyfriend died and never finished it and the postcard was just a postcard and the hole was just a hole. Maybe the hotel was just a crummy old hotel lucky to be torn down. Maybe none of it was connected, after all.

Maybe, maybe, maybe.

But here was Grandma's writing on the page: *your Marnie forever.* And here was Nick talking about a postcard. And here — right in my hands — was a postcard with a tiny light saying, "Look here! Look here!"

The more I looked through the pinhole, and the more I knew that I was free of Mom and Dad for a few days, the more I realized I was wondering just how to get to the Hotel DeSoto.

CHAPTER TWENTY

It was another sunny day in the Sunshine City when I woke. Mrs. K served watery eggs for breakfast, sunny-side up, of course. While she was making them, I glanced around for mail or magazines with her name on the subscription label. No luck.

"I'm going to keep working until the hospital opens," I told her.

"Let me know when, and I'll get us a taxi," she said.

I wasn't sure how I would deal with that, but I went back to my house and started cleaning up, tossing three ratty folding chairs into the Dumpster, along with two old mattresses from the garage and a dozen broken garden pots and brittle plastic rakes from the shed. Big rolling trash cans were out and full all along the street, so I emptied two garbage bags of trash into our can and rolled it to the end of the driveway. I swept and hosed the patio and sponged the kitchen counter, too. There, I did some house cleaning. What a good son. And grandson.

I heard the sound of a mower and saw Dia cutting another lawn down the street. Maybe her own, for a change. I had to talk to her about finishing our grass, but I wasn't ready yet. Besides, I was thinking of only one thing. Visiting hours started at ten. I had, give or take, two hours before my father would wonder where I was. I didn't think I would need that long.

Wait? Was I still thinking of actually *going* to the Hotel DeSoto? Hadn't I complained to Hector that everyone here was nuts? Was it happening to me now?

I stood unmoving over Grandma's desk. I hadn't managed to call Randy Halbert yet, so he'd probably come over soon. The house was still a mess, no matter what I'd done. Dad was in the hospital, for crying out loud. Family Services might come any moment. Forget it!

Besides, did I really care about this old postcard? Grandma was gone. The pinhole could have gotten there for any reason. And the **II**. Even if the card actually was a clue, what was it a clue *to*? Chapter II of the story? Yeah, right. I would find that after sixty years. Not to mention that the writer was already dead. Not to mention that the hotel was being demolished, so I'd never get close to it, anyway. It'd been sixty years. Sixty years! Come on!

Through the back window I saw Mrs. K hanging laundry. The air smelled of heat and lemon blossoms and clean wet clothes. Sunlight slanted down through the trees to the backyard, lighting up the grass as if it were under a spotlight. It wasn't quite the same lime green as on the postcard, but it was close. The dark undersides of the palm leaves swayed, and their sharp leaves, stringy where they had dried and strips had pealed off, clattered in the breeze. The trunks sat like fat elephant legs.

"Whatever." I breathed out loud. "It's stupid. I'm going to the hospital."

The hospital. I thought about Dad lying there all busted up. He had come down to Florida to bury his mother. He did it, and now what? He needed something, didn't he? Besides her dying and his broken leg and banged-up head and closing up her house and going back to Boston and to Mom. Was that all there was now? Sell the house and go back?

In the hospital, he had started to say something.

He had said: ". . . without her . . . I feel . . ."

He didn't finish. But I knew what he was going to say. Empty. "Without her . . . I feel . . . empty."

I opened my backpack, took out the pajamas and toothbrush, slipped in the card and the magazine, and cinched it closed.

"So . . . I'm going to the hotel?" I asked the room.

"I'm going." I had two hours. I could go and be back in time to be at the hospital when visiting hours began. Then I could tell Dad: "I'm trying to reach Mom, but hey, you remember that funny old postcard? I know it was nothing, but I followed up on it. It turned out to be nothing, too, but hey, you never know." I think he would actually like that I did it. It would be something of his own about Grandma. Mine, a little. Ours, a little. But mostly his.

I made sure the back door was locked. I checked if Mrs. K was still out there, didn't see her, then went to the front door and slipped out quietly.

CHAPTER TWENTY-ONE

Tried to slip out quietly.

"There you are, dear!"

Crud. Mrs. K was in the front yard now. Man, she moved fast! She was on her knees in the flowers by her lamppost, a little trowel dangling from her gloved hand. "Hospital time? I'll get my bag."

It just came to me. "No. It's early. And you don't have to. Dia . . ."

She looked at me blankly. "Dia?"

"Dia . . . is coming . . . with me," I said. "She wanted to come with me. On the bus."

What? Where did that come from? I amazed myself with how fully I was into the truth-bending thing (which now seemed a lot more like lying).

Mrs. K looked confused. "Dia?" she repeated.

"The lawn mower girl. The girl who mows our lawn? Dia Martin. I'm going to Dia's house now," I said, using her name in a polite way, to make Mrs. K think I was polite.

"Oh. Are you sure?"

I smiled. "Yes. She's waiting for me."

"Will I see you for dinner?"

"Definitely," I said. "It's a date."

"Don't forget to leave lights on," she said.

"It's kind of early for that, isn't it?" I said.

"You never know."

"Okay. I will." I turned, then turned back. "And thanks. For taking care of me."

"You're welcome, dear. Say hello to your father." She smiled and plunged her trowel into the dirt at the base of the lamppost.

I had done it. Three minutes later, I was on my way to the bus stop. Dia was now in somebody's side yard blowing up an inflatable pool for some small kids who were jumping up and down around her. They didn't look like her brothers or sisters, so I guessed she was babysitting. I still had to talk to her about finishing the grass, but maybe now wasn't the time. She caught my eye, made as if she was going to say something, probably remembered what a dork I had been and how I had shooed her away from my yard, then made a face and looked away.

Yeah, sorry, I thought. *I should have minded my own business when you were cutting our grass. Maybe Dad wouldn't have yelled at me.*

Never mind. He was sad. He'd been drinking. He's not going to do that anymore. Enough. "Enuf!" I said.

I passed on to the corner, looking back once to see her following me with her eyes, her cheeks puffing out from behind the growing plastic pool. I found the right bus from the map at the stop and minutes later was on my way downtown.

It's not like I was going *into* the hotel! I wouldn't actually be able to go where the pinhole pointed, since it was on the top floor, but so what? I was just going to look at the place. It would be crawling with workers. I would walk by. Notice stuff. Then I'd show Dad the clues I found on the postcard and wasn't that strange? He'd like how it was all about Grandma. I think it would mean something to him. Then I'd tell him about the cleaning up I had done. Perfect.

The moment I got off the bus, I was sticky again. The perspiration dripped down my eyebrows and into the corners of my eyes. It stung as if someone had sprayed Windex in my face. I also had the feeling someone was watching me, but who even knew I was here? Maybe just a kid on his own was strange.

I walked a few blocks from the bus stop toward the Pier, until I stopped at the corner of Central Avenue and 2nd Street.

And there it was. The Hotel DeSoto. A strange thrill went through me as I pictured young Nicky Falcon and his father on the sidewalk in front of it. Surprisingly, the hotel still looked a lot like it did on the postcard. It was surrounded by a high chain-link fence now, but it was still standing in its own proud sort of way. As if it had survived a lot of years, and even now it wouldn't just crumble away to dust, not yet.

I held my breath as I moved along the opposite sidewalk to where the photographer must have been standing, then matched the card against the actual building. One of the trees was much bigger than on the card. The other had been cut down. There had also been some construction since the picture was taken. The card was sixty years old, after all. The patio was gone. The short wall in front of the courtyard was gone. The red awning, gone. For some reason, that struck me. I liked imagining the sound of the breeze making the canvas squeak.

The sidewalk in front of the hotel was chewed up, too. Wired onto the fence was a large poster with a computer sketch of the luxury mall that was going up. The DeSoto Galleria.

Normally, I wouldn't mind that. Normally, I would say, "Mall? Yay!" But I didn't like this. Whatever else the postcard might mean, here was a piece of the past being taken away, and it struck me as not a good thing. I thought of the lobby in Emerson Beale's story, the mahogony counter, the tufted cushions, the gold-painted columns. Had those things already been taken away? Had they ever been there in the first place?

A half dozen workmen came out the front doors of the hotel, locked the fence behind them, and walked to the corner. I found myself wondering if the hotel was empty now.

"What? I'm not actually going in. I can't go *in* the hotel."

Then why was I already starting to cross Central Avenue? No way. I stepped back to the sidewalk. A policeman slowed his car at the opposite corner, pulled over, and called to the man who had closed the fence. There was some shouting and a laugh. Then the light changed. Cars went by. There was another laugh, then a slap on the roof of the car, and the policeman drove away while the workmen headed into a coffee shop.

The light changed, and I crossed the avenue to the other side. I walked casually down the sidewalk in front of the hotel, then stopped to look up at the whole thing.

A yellow caution tape was knotted here and there along the fence, and a No Admittance sign hung on the gate the workers had come out of.

"This is dumb," I said to myself. Dumb or not, my heart was racing, and the hair on the back of my neck was bristling.

I felt the texture of the postcard between my fingers, glanced at it, looked both ways, saw no one in particular, and slipped under the caution tape.

I slipped under the caution tape! I could have ducked back under it again and walked to the corner and then gone to visit Dad in the hospital, but I didn't. I eased my way to where the fence passed the tree and in two steps was up over it and onto the tree's lowest branch. I dropped down on the inside.

Hurrying to the hotel's double doors, I looked behind me, still saw no one watching, then slid between the doors and into the lobby.

CHAPTER TWENTY-TWO

The giant open room was hushed and hot and seemed to pull me deep into it with my first step. The sound of the street outside grew muffled and distant.

I gulped for air as if I were trying to swallow the whole room. The only light was from high narrow windows facing the street and were still draped with thick green curtains. It felt like the land of the dead in there.

A few pieces of old furniture were scattered around the lobby. Two soiled sofas of what had once been lime green. A half dozen battered chairs, ripped and stained and sunken. The counter of old polished wood was still visible under a giant paint-splattered canvas sheet. There were stacks of wall trim and molding by the front doors. Sledgehammers were leaning here and there against the walls or on the floor amid electric saws and crowbars and tool chests. The ceiling plaster had crumbled and was lying in gilded chunks around the floor. An elevated machine braced up the ceiling to keep the rest of it from falling, because the massive columns were lying side by side on the floor like giant sticks of chalk, strapped together with bands of steel. Maybe they were going to be saved?

A smell of something earthy caught my nose. Two potted palms, dead and brown, lay on their sides, their soil splashed out and mixing with the rest of the rubble.

Off the left of the lobby behind the registration area and next to the elevator were stairs leading to the upper floors. It was on those stairs that Nick Falcon had first seen the kid he later called Mr. Tall loping down from the floor above. Had he really become the weirdly tall man I'd seen at the funeral? A second caution tape was strung loosely across from the registration desk to the stairs. It was all pretty ghostly. The smell of age and dust and must and mold was everywhere, but the lobby *was* like Beale had written about it.

Okay, I've done it. I was going now. The workmen . . .

I turned toward the doors and saw where Nicky might have stumbled in that day to see Marnie. *A single willow.* Nearby were the remains of what I guessed was the newspaper rack that Nick's father had sent him in to check. Now it was no more than slats of wood and shelves lining a broken stand.

I paused. "Hey, Nicky," I whispered to the quiet, dusty room. "They're tearing it down, where you first saw her. The morons."

I went to the stand and ran my finger over the dusty plank. It shone like polished oak.

Without knowing I was moving, I found myself standing at the bottom of the stairs. Ducking under the tape, I started up.

Jeez! Jeez! Will you stop?

I didn't. Three flights I went up, one after another after another, around and around and around until I was standing in the hallway of the top floor, my heart pounding against my ribs, my ears burning.

If it was ghostly and quiet downstairs, it was as silent as a tomb up there. I looked at the postcard, imagined the floor plan, and went left to a corner, then right. The carpet was still down, though here and there worn all the way to the wood. The floorboards creaked with every step. Most of the room doors were open. Some rooms were in shambles, others empty, some with the skeletons of bed frames, others with small tables and broken chairs, and all of them thick with dust. People had lived here once. Were they all dead now?

I stopped. Did I really think I'd find Chapter II of the story? Sixty years later? Was it a trap? Was it nothing?

What the heck am I doing here?

Five times I turned back toward the stairs. Five times I turned again and kept walking, each time a little farther than before. When I reached the end of the hallway, I peeked through the narrow crack of the last door. Inside I saw two windows, one on each wall. I looked at the postcard again.

Okay, then.

I was there.

I pushed the door open.

S.83—Alligators in Tropical Florida
Sarasota Jungle Gardens   3C-H959

CHAPTER TWENTY-THREE

My breath caught in my throat when the door swung all the way in and tapped the inside wall. Sunlight sliced through the blinds at a sharp angle onto the bare floor. The room was empty except for a coating of plaster dust everywhere. I don't know what I was thinking, but I pulled on the door behind me, then watched as it closed nearly all the way.

I tilted the blinds and looked out.

People crisscrossed the street below. Cars drove by. On the spot where I had been looking up at the room, a man and a woman stood smoking outside an office. He waved his arms, she nodded, then he nodded. A few moments later, they checked their watches, tamped out their cigarettes, and went back inside. They reminded me of the fat man with the silver cigarette case. And the lobby downstairs. And all the steps that had brought me to this room.

The day was going on outside. But inside the old hotel it was like a grave. No, not that. A grave is still, unmoving. I knew about graves. I had just seen one. Being in this room was like standing in a kind of space that — now that I had come — was moving slowly but surely away from the street, away from the city. Away from the present.

I closed the blinds. The air was so heavy and close. I stood for a long time, just sucking in breaths.

What would I say if I were caught? Even if I weren't, what would I say about this? A sudden thrill went through me. I realized I was both nervous and excited. That feeling spiked and faded, and then I felt sick to my stomach.

You're breaking the law, doofus. Get out of here.

I didn't move.

Think about it. The workmen will be back any second. Get out —

I didn't move much then, either, but I did turn. That was when I saw the bathroom door. It was open a crack. And as dim as the main room was, the bathroom was beaming in full morning light. I guessed there were no blinds on the window. I lifted the card close and found the pinhole again.

It's in the bathroom.

I walked into the little room. It was empty. The fixtures were gone, their pipes sticking out of the wall. Black-and-white tiles covered the floor. I actually searched all around the window with my hands, then all around the walls for hollow places, knocking at the plaster walls the way they do in movies. Nothing. It was just an empty bathroom waiting to be destroyed. There was nothing else.

Of course, there was nothing else!

It was when I stepped away from the window and turned that I saw an iron grate, low on the wall under the sink pipes. Maybe it was where the heat came in. Or . . .

I turned the card over and saw once more the tiny dots under the two words. I breathed out. "Or air conditioning."

Trembling, I knelt to the wall. Putting my fingers through the holes in the grate, I pulled on it. It didn't give.

Four screws held it in place. I searched the room until I found a loose nail.

Dad, Dad, you'll never guess what I did this morning —

I slotted the nailhead into one screw and turned. It began to loosen. Every few seconds, I listened for sounds below me. Hearing none, I kept on. After I removed the third screw, the grate swung down from the wall shaft behind it. I put my hands in.

The shaft was lined in metal and went straight down behind the wall to the floor below. A foot or so below the level of the opening I felt what I first thought was a narrow shelf. Only it wasn't a shelf, because my fingers felt hinges on the angle nearest the inside wall. Feeling all around it, I discovered that it was shaped like a shallow box. Carefully, I pressed it this way and that and — *snap!* — it came off the wall into my hands. What I pulled up out of the shaft was a metal box an inch deep, hinged, but not locked.

I set it on the bathroom floor and gently opened it.

I fell back on my butt. Sitting inside the box was a large brown envelope.

You've got to be kidding me. . . .

The envelope was ripped and filthy, and part of the label was torn off, but I could tell that it was addressed to someone named C. H. Dobbs on 52nd Street. It was post-marked from Singapore.

Dobbs? What the heck . . . ! I took the magazine from my backpack and read the contents. "Dying the Hard Way," by Chester H. Dobbs, was one of the stories.

I lifted the envelope up out of the box and opened the flap. Inside was a thin stack of paper covered with words in thick, clogged typewriter type. My hands were shaking like the hands of a sick man. I couldn't believe what I read at the top of the first page.

– II –

THE LONG WAY BACK
By Emerson Beale

I could barely breathe. There must have been twenty pages in all. Making sure I had everything, I replaced the grate, tightened the screws (quite a trick with my quivering hands), and scuttled back to the main room.

I headed for the door, but my eyes couldn't stop scanning the words on the first page. The hotel was so silent, I stopped. I knew I needed to be gone, to be out of there and far away, but I also knew I couldn't move until I read a few words. The first page, no more.

Without thinking how a dead man could write a story, I slid down the wall under the window. Its light slanted across the yellowed paper, and I began to read.

4A-H806

CHAPTER TWENTY-FOUR

— II —

THE LONG WAY BACK
By Emerson Beale

Two weeks after popping out of the blue sedan's trunk like a cheap magician, I was strolling on a street near the Pier when someone played marimba on my head with a blackjack.

I woke up who knows how many hours later trussed in a marlin net on the deck of a filthy boat. There was a bump on my head the size of a bowling ball.

I felt sick all over as if I'd been battered with shovels.

Maybe I was dead.

Maybe I was dead and maybe angels sail you to heaven in stinking fishing boats. But I doubted it.

The smell of the water and the black of the sky and the tiny lights far off told me it was deep in the night, the water was shallow, and we were chugging toward shore.

Two dim shapes stood over me. Not angels. A match flashing onto a cigarette revealed my old yellow-socked friend, Mr. Bones. The redbearded Nazi was planted next to him like a dwarf palm.

"An enemy is what you made for yourself," Mr. Bones growled. "But don't get your head too swelled. Some people get Fang mad just by breathing."

"Fang?" I said, remembering the fat man's teeth. "Figures. Is he your boss?"

"Yours, too. Only you don't know it right," he said.

"Fang is Marnie Blaine's father?" I said.

"Correck!" Redbeard snapped helpfully.

"What does he want me to do?"

Yellow Socks laughed until he doubled over at the waist, as if he were hinged. "Do? Two things. First, Fang wants you to die. When you're all done doing that, he wants you to come back to see his daughter just about never."

"Neffer!" echoed the tubby German.

"Can you be a little more clear?" I asked.

"Ess clear ess a khost!" said Redbeard, wagging an ugly curved dagger at my waist, then my knees, then my chest, then my head, as if it were some kind of pencil, and he was going to draw me with it.

"You see, Falcon, Fang wants to know only one thing about you," said Skull.

"And what's that?"

"Fang wants to know that the next time you talk to his daughter, you're dead."

It was that speaking style again. I had to hand it to the guy. It was different. All through his little speech his dead smile didn't change, though his eyes went a little more icy. When he raised his hand to his shoulder and tapped it three times, there came a sudden rapid thwacking from the night air. A burst of wild color fluttered out of it and settled on his coat. It was a parrot.

"Fang! Fang!" it shrieked. *"Fanggggg!"*

"You fellows know how truly odd this looks, don't you?" I said. "Maybe I should leave you to your little show and be on my way. I have to feed my mongoose —"

Skeleton's shoe hiked up my shoulder. He then made a bad impression of someone laughing.

"Do it! It!" he commanded, and Herr Beardbarrel lunged at me with his dagger. But not to kill me. He sliced me out of the marlin net at the same time as Skull whipped out again, with his fist this time, and clocked me on the chin. I tumbled out of the boat and into the water. *Splash!* Luckily, it wasn't deep.

"You like a mystery, boy. Well, figure where you are now!" Skull snarled as he spun the wheel and drove the boat away. "Heh, heh!"

I staggered to my feet. "I'll be back, you know. Marnie will know—"

"That dead is what you are? We'll deliver the message!"

"Ze messedge!" Redbeard repeated. Then they both hollered, "Heh, heh, heh!" Their cries echoed deep into the still marshes and in my ears long after the sound of the boat had vanished.

I thought, "They just want to scare me, do they? They want to teach me to stay away from the girl? Make me a little wet, a little uncomfortable? Okay, I get it."

Nuh-uh. It was a bigger than that. My eyes were getting used to the dark now, and I looked around. As Skullhead had said, I did like a mystery, but it was no mystery where he and his pal had dumped me. Coiled roots stretching across the water like dead fingers grasping for life. Water as black as a sea in Hades. The smell of rotting mangrove trees.

"The Everglades!"

Too bad I didn't have time to thank the thugs for the complimentary boat ride. There came a faint *scooo*... then a sudden watery sound, a slithering splash, and a breathy growl in the black marsh to my left. I cocked my head. I knew those sounds. They were the calling cards of an alligator, sliding off a mudbank and into the water. Except that when the moonlight glinted off its armored hide, this one turned out to be the largest alligator I'd ever seen. Fifteen feet from snout to tail and a half ton of hungry meanness.

I let the muck suck my shoes off and sloshed quickly to one of the mangrove trees, which I crawled up and jumped at until I grasped a branch. I snapped it off. How it happened is a mystery, but the gator's first attack — it launched itself like a torpedo across the swamp — didn't kill me. I whomped the branch on its nose and staggered free. The breath of a thousand tiny wings sounded among the swamp. Hummingbirds! Their whirring was like a glimmering thread of light through the darkness. I imagined Marnie's voice leading me to safety. I followed. The chomping jaws were seconds behind me. I would have been footless, legless, lifeless in no time, but for those wings and that stick.

"Get back!" I yelled, trying to engage the gator in conversation. "Not talking, eh?" I swung the branch like a baseball bat and caught it between the gator's jaws as they clamped down.

Unbelievably, the limb didn't crack. The gator's teeth sank into the wood and stuck in them for half a second. It was the half second I needed.

Using its head as a diving board, I launched myself into the marsh, crawled up the side of a mangrove trunk as far as I could go, and clung to its branches. For six hours I cooled my heels until well past dawn, when the sun, hot and full and close, lulled the beast to sleep. I climbed down and crept away.

Too bad that wasn't the end of it. After resting up a week in a little place on Key West, I crawled back to St. Petersburg to confront Fang. I never got close. His minions made sure of that. I saw Marnie once, but only for a second before Skull finally made good on his threat to make an appointment for me. But not with the doctor.

This time it was a travel agent.

When I came to, if you can call it that, my hands were tied with something thick and rough. A wad of oily-tasting rags was crammed into my mouth, and my eyes were squeezed shut behind a blindfold of scratchy wool. I rolled slowly back and forth with the slowly tilting floor.

Where was I?

The constant sound of an engine rumbling and the back-and-forth movement told me I was on another boat. But this one was big. An oil tanker, if I smelled right. An hour later, I'd uncovered one eye and spat out the rag.

The hatch opened, and a short crewman swayed in. He had a nasty look on his face and a nastier wrench in his hand.

"Why am I here?" I demanded.

He looked me up and down.

"Ever hear of the Order, boy?"

"Order? Sure, coffee and a sinker, coming up!"

He tested his wrench against my head, and the wrench won. I went right down. I just had time to hear him — or someone — say a word before I blacked out and struck the floor.

It sounded like, "Oobarab."

A day later, or maybe it was a week, I heard the engines stop. The great iron vessel hung motionless in the water. I wobbled to my feet when the hull rocked suddenly, and I was down again. "Thanks a lot," I grumbled.

Then there was another shudder, louder this time, then water rushing and men shouting.

A crewman, not the same one, charged into the hold, saw me, stumbled over, and cut my bonds. "The Japanese are attacking!" he yelled. "Get the hell off this ship!"

"The Japanese! Off the Florida coast?"

"You dimwit!" he snarled. "You been out longer than you thought. You're off Singapore now, boy!"

A third explosion buffeted the tanker, and I knew it was the big one. We took on water and listed to starboard. I crawled up the stairway amid a hail of machine-gun fire and concussions in the air and below the surface. By the time I got to the top, the ship was so far over, the stairs were horizontal. I stepped off the top rung and sank into the water.

To make a long story short, a Navy cruiser raced into the area, the Japanese were driven off, and we were rescued. Two weeks after that, I was in the Army.

Damn the bum eye. I found a troop of soldiers on leave, asked to meet their commanding officer, and enlisted right then and there. I'd say I faked my way through the exam, but they weren't fussy with the reading chart. They needed me.

"Welcome, Nick," said a soldier whose platoon I got

into. "I'm Private R. F. Fracker. But you can call me Freddie. Nice to meet you, pal."

I dropped the pages. "Fracker? Fracker! Oh my gosh! Dad! The lawyer! What the ——!" I snatched up the pages again.

I made quick friends with Freddie. It had to be quick. I knew him only long enough to discover he was an okay guy, alone in the world, with no family, before he gave all he had for his country. Less than a month into my service, we were landing swift and hard on a crummy little island called Saipan. We just had time to tighten our helmet straps when we were ambushed in a jungle clearing. Forty-five minutes later, I was holding Freddie's chest together with my hands.

"Listen, Nick," he said, barely getting the words out, "watch yourself —"

"Don't try to talk," I said. "A medic's coming."

That was a lie. No one was coming.

"Look," he said. "The short guy. Curtis. He's been eyeing you. Don't know what his beef is. Nick, he seemed mighty interested when he heard your name. 'Falcon?' he says. 'Farmers shoot falcons.' 'So what?' I says. 'So maybe I'm a farmer,' he says. Nick, I think he's choosing his time to get you alone. I've tried to watch out for you, but I think I'll be checking out soon."

"You won't —"

"Don't kid me," he said, holding up a bloody hand. "I left my insides in the clearing somewhere. I expect I'll collect them before I leave. They say you're whole again when you fly up to heaven. Looks like you could use the medic for your shoulder. He won't of come for nothing."

I tried to stifle what I was feeling, but it came out anyway, and I began to blubber. "Freddie —"

"Shut up, Nick. And thanks for everything," he said, more softly now. With an effort he could hardly afford, he opened his collar and ripped the dog tags off his neck. He pressed them into my hand. "Nice coupla weeks, huh? Open the eyes on the back of your head, Nicky. And go find your Marnie."

He didn't talk for a while after that. Exhausted and bleeding from my shoulder, I passed out. When I came to, he had died. It was as simple as that.

They patched me up. Not three days later, in another jungle — or was it the same one? — I turned and found myself staring down the barrel of an M1 Garand. The face behind it, squinting and angry, was Curtis's.

"I gotta do it, you —!" He swore. "I know something about you."

"Yeah?"

"People don't like the people you been talking to—"

My mind reeled. "Curtis, put the rifle down."

"Oobarab told me, and I gotta do it!"

"Oobarab? That's the second time—"

"The Order told me to, and I gotta."

"Wait, who's Ooba—"

In one of those moments that stay with you no matter how long you live, I saw his trigger finger tighten ever so slowly. "Oh, gawww—!"

There was a deafening *boom,* and Curtis flew up into the air, screaming. It seemed like he went away in different directions at the same time. Something wet splashed my face, my eyes; my head fell back; I was out.

I was shaking all over. The slatted light from the blinds was cutting across the pages now. I couldn't go on, for right where my fingers held the page his name was written in the margin in the same blue ink as before. *Emerson.* Beside it was a date: *July 14.* On the top of the next page was his name again, written in pencil and traced over a few times with black pen, then blue pen until it was pretty thick. There were two dates there. *Septem. 2, 1947,* and *Novemb. 5.* I quickly flipped through the rest of the pages, but that was the last mark my grandmother made.

I didn't know what that meant. I kept on reading.

"What day is it?" I asked.

"Day?" The man laughed. "Try year, my lad. It's been nearly eighteen months since you were discharged into my care. And that, after a year in the Army hospital."

He tossed me a newspaper.

I read the date through my bandages. "1947!"

Turns out, after the blast on Saipan, I had been in a coma, then in and out of consciousness for quite a while. Infection after infection in between bouts of hallucination and delirium kept me in beds and bandages for thirteen months. When the Army needed my cot for some sap worse off than me, they booted me out, mummy-faced, half crazy, half dead. Without knowing it, I'd been laying up in a flea-ridden hotel near the Singapore harbor run by an old Englishman named Harrow who'd taken pity on me. It was a third-floor walkup in a fifth-rate joint with a bed, a desk, a typewriter, and what sounded like a rat the size of a terrier living rent-free inside the walls.

Harrow had been a doctor, first in London, then Madrid, then Bombay, before he finally switched careers and became a drunk. He was the only Harley Street man in all of Congo for a time, where he sometimes counted his wages in donkeys and elephants and pack dogs.

Whatever his past, he still knew a thing or two about face wounds, and he was a regular expert with anesthesia. He had a whole cabinet of the stuff.

It wasn't a bad place, after all. Every morning I woke to a fat orange sun, mad parrots squawking in the street markets, and Harrow's tales of village doctoring. Every day I worked on writing this story. And every morning, noon, night, and each second in between, I thought of Marnie.

Whenever I closed my eyes, her face was there. It almost struck me as funny that here I was with maybe no face at all, and all I could think of was her's. But love is like that.

One hot afternoon, the first time I refused my daily anesthesia, Harrow put down the tray and said, "Well, then, old fellow, I think it's time. Shall we see how mangled you are?"

I looked up from the typewriter.

"Singapore is scary enough," I said. "You sure —"

"I have to," he said grimly. "A little matter of a prescription I wrote for a local...well, let's call him a businessman. The fellow had a bad reaction to it. Killed him. I hear his family is taking a stroll here now."

I tensed. "Maybe they're just shopping for answers?"

"I think we're rather beyond the answer stage now," he said. "They're shopping for something else. And since I've grown fond of my head, I'm taking it to Hong Kong. But there's a steamer in port that might interest you. It's heading for San Diego in a day or two. Last time I checked, that's in the States. Besides that..." He paused.

"What?"

He breathed heavily. "Nineteen years in Singapore has taught me a fair amount of the Malay and Tamil dialects. But one word they use I've never heard before."

A shiver went up my neck. "Not...Oobarab?"

He smirked. "So you speak the same language. They talked of some 'Secret Order.' Didn't sound like a welcoming sort of club."

I closed my eyes and tried to follow the train of connections. From the Everglades to Japan to Singapore, from Fang to Curtis to a local gang of killers. "Then we're both on borrowed time."

"Yes, Nicky, I believe so." He looked at his watch. "Now, come. Let's take a look, eh?"

He closed the blinds and the room went purple. He unfolded a mirror from his pocket and stood it on the desk. I noticed that either the parrots had stopped chattering in the street or everything had gone quiet in my head.

I stared into the mirror as he unwound my bandages slowly and gently. When he pulled the last damp swath off, my breath caught in my throat, and I screamed.

The parrots started cackling again.

— Jan. 1947

Continued in Chapter III

CHAPTER TWENTY-FIVE

I stopped reading. My pulse was going a mile a minute.

So . . . he lived? This is so unbe —

A sound came from the stairway.

I swear my heart died right then and there. I froze where I sat, trying not to make a sound. Someone was coming for me, walking down the hall right now. I crawled silently into the bathroom and squeezed the door shut.

Someone entered the room. I could hear the crunch of plaster dust on the floor as the steps made their way one by one to the window. They turned. Another crunch.

I was shaking, sweating, shaking, soaking wet. Please, no, no.

The bathroom door swung open.

"Ahhhh!" I screamed.

"Oh, could you not? I've just spent an hour with shrieking kids."

"Ahhhh!" I screamed again, then slumped down to the tiles. It was Dia, the lawn mower girl. "What the holy —"

"That's nice language."

"What are you *doing* here?" I said.

She made a face. "I figured since shuffleboard was canceled, we could play canasta. I even brought cards!"

It didn't compute. "What are you talking about?"

"I followed you, Barney! It's St. Petersburg. I'm under eighty. What else was there for me to do?"

"What the . . . okay, first, how did you know I was here? And how did you even get here?"

She smiled over-sweetly. "I asked Daddy to follow your bus. You were being all weird, not talking to me and slinking off to the bus stop, looking over your shoulder. You'd make such a lousy spy, by the way. So I told Daddy, and we followed. He's always up for stuff. We saw you get off and come in here. He said it wasn't safe for you, so I said I'd get you out. He trusts me. I had to search every floor to find you."

"Wait. How could your father just do that?"

"Do what?"

"Drop you off in the middle of downtown all alone?"

She rolled her eyes up. "Come on. I'm not dumb. I know downtown. Besides, he's parked right out front. Plus, I have a cell phone right here if I need it" — she tapped my pants pocket with her shoe, *my* pocket! — "which I don't, because there are two of us now."

I looked up at her a long time with what I guess was a blank look. Only after a while did it strike me that because she was there, my lying to Mrs. K was back to bending the truth. Dia and I *were* together. We just hadn't *come* together. It wasn't the hospital, of course, but it was somewhere. I guess I grinned to myself about that, but it was the wrong thing to do. Dia must have thought I glimpsed the outline of her bathing suit under her T-shirt (which I guess I did) and she spun around quickly toward the door.

"So . . . what's for room service?"

I staggered to my feet and followed her into the main room. "The hotel is condemned. They don't have —" I stopped. "Wait. What about the kids?"

"What kids?"

"The kids you were babysitting?"

She jumped. "Oh my God! I left them in the pool! They can't swim. Nooooo!"

I panicked. "Are you crazy!"

She gave me another look. "Yeah, because I do that. I follow weirdos to condemned hotels when I'm supposed to save little kids from drowning. Their mom is with them, Einstein. I only went over to help her blow up the pool for them. Yeah, if you can believe that. 'Help her.' I blew the whole thing up while she stirred lemonade in the kitchen. By the time she came out all perky I had lost a lung. Then I came here. All right, Popeye?"

"It's Jason."

"Uh-huh," she said, running her fingers along the plaster dust of the window sill. "But, look. We all know why I'm here. Why are you here? What do you have there? And finally, why are you here?"

I couldn't think of any reason not to, so . . . I told her . . . everything.

I showed her the magazine. I told her about Grandma. Her boyfriend who supposedly died in Japan. The phone call. The hotel. The real estate agent. My dad's accident.

The postcard. The little hole. Even my father's lawyer friend who also supposedly died in Japan.

It must have sounded confused and jumbled up and backward all the way until I showed her the grate on the bathroom wall and the envelope I had found. I blabbed through it in about three minutes. She stood there the whole time with her mouth hanging open. I finished with the word, "Oobarab."

"I get it," she said. "I really do. This weird guy writes a weird story in which he mentions a weird clue in a postcard and then goes missing. And suddenly your grammy gets a postcard. And suddenly you find more of the weird story."

"But I think there's a real mystery here," I said. "Emerson Beale is supposed to be dead by the time Grandma gets the postcard. But he didn't die like the editor's note in the magazine said he did. These pages tell how he actually survived —"

"Wait," she said, "the real guy or the fake character?"

I frowned. "Well, both, I think. He was wounded and his face changed and he lived and wrote this story. And the guy who died in the story is really alive and is someone my father knew!"

I had the feeling I was saying everything twice so that she would understand, but I finally ran out of words.

She was down on the floor now and looking first at the magazine, then at the pages of Chapter II one after another. It was a minute or two before she spoke. Finally, she said, "Whatever these pages are, your grandma knew they were hidden here in this hotel. She obviously came back to them a few times. She wrote on the pages at different times and in different color inks." She tapped the pages. "She came here a lot. To reread this story."

"Okay."

"So then you've gotta wonder . . . *why?*"

"*Why?*" I repeated. "Because she liked him. Emerson Beale."

"Not that. I mean *why* is the story still here? If the postcard actually *was* a clue, which it was, and she found the story here and read it a bunch of times, which we know she did from her dates on the pages, then why didn't she just take the story with her? Why did she keep it hidden here? And why could we still find it here sixty years later?"

I frowned. I hadn't thought of that. "I don't know. But besides, *I* found it."

She wagged her head for a little while. "So okay, I don't know why it's still here, either. But I think . . . maybe . . . I have to . . . go to the bathroom."

"What?"

"I said I have to —"

Thump.

We froze. Someone was coming. Someone real, this time. Not a lawn-mowing babysitter. The blood in my veins went ice cold.

"Please tell me that's your dad," I whispered.

Thump.

"About that," she said, shaking her head. "I sort of lied. He's already gone to work in Tampa."

"Are you kidding?"

"Shhh!"

"Oh my gosh —" I swallowed my words. I snatched the pages back, stuffed them into the envelope, and put it in my backpack.

Scrape. Thump. Scrape. Thump.

"Limper!" she said.

"Who's Limper?" I asked.

"A person who limps! Let's beat him!"

"Beat him?" I said. "Are you nuts?"

"I mean in a race, you dork! Do they hit invalids in Boston?"

Before I could answer, she dragged me out to the hallway, and we ran.

Gandy Bridge, Six Miles Long, Between Tampa and St. Petersburg, Florida

P-106

CHAPTER TWENTY-SIX

And I mean we *ran*. We climbed out a side window and jumped onto the fire escape just as the work crew poured out of the coffee shop.

"Hey! You kids! Get offa that. It's not safe!" they shouted when they saw us on the stairs. The rusty stairs quivered as we went down and began to pull away from the wall. We managed to scramble to street level before anything happened and dashed into a side alley — a cut-through! — blocked by the fence. We tore off down a back street and didn't stop for three and a half blocks. Dia said she *really* had to go to the bathroom now. She lurched into a store, and I followed her. It was a flower shop.

Breathless, scanning out the window for any signs of the workmen, I saw a police car drive by. It was going slow. The same officer as before was inside. One of the workmen was hanging out the car window, gawking up and down the street. I ducked behind a big bouquet of flowers and peeked. I watched the tail end of the car continue through the next light. I should have relaxed, but my brain was still racing.

What did I get myself into?

Spanish music jangled on the radio. The only word I heard was *colibri . . . colibri* which made me wonder if *Oobarab* was a Spanish word, though it didn't sound like it. Then I thought of the word *libro,* which I knew was *book* in Spanish, and I thought of *co libro,* which might mean a book written by two people or about two people, and I thought about the story in my backpack right then and wondered: if Emerson Beale *did* live, did it mean maybe he and my grandmother . . . got together? It still almost didn't matter because we were talking fifteen years before my dad was born.

The woman behind the counter smiled at me and said something fast in Spanish, when Dia came out of the back room.

"Whew!" she said. "That was close."

"No kidding," I said. "The police just drove by."

"No, I mean me. Man!"

"Policia?" said the woman at the counter, suddenly interested.

Dia laughed — it was like a bell chiming in that tight flowery place. She said something apologetic in more quick Spanish. The counter lady shrugged and sat back on her stool.

By that time, the streets looked pretty clear of police, so we left the shop. We walked the side streets and got farther away from the hotel.

"Okay," I said finally. "There was somebody else in there with us. Not the workers. Someone else."

"Someone who limps and is not very fast," she said. "Which was lucky for us because you run like a girl."

I looked at her. "What?"

"It's okay," she said. "I used to also."

I breathed out. "Anyway, somebody knew we were there. And they were after us."

"After you," she said. "Or the story." She tapped my backpack.

The whole mystery — if it even *was* a mystery — was

as muddy in my mind as the swamp on that magazine cover. I tried to get it all out loud. "Let's forget everything else and suppose that my grandma and Emerson Beale are Nick Falcon and Marnie Blaine. Or the other way around. And Nick or Emerson, or whoever, is forbidden to see her. Fang is this bad guy who is like Grandma's father, but not exactly, because he probably didn't actually have abnormally long teeth. He sends his goon guys to get rid of him."

"Uh-huh, because that happens," she said.

"Whatever. It's in the story. Besides, my dad said her father actually *didn't* like him. But in the story there's some kind of secret outfit that works for Fang, and they kidnap Nick."

"The Secret Order of Scooby-Doo," she said.

"Oobarab."

"Only Nick escapes," she went on. "He's in World War II, and he gets wounded. But he doesn't die. But everybody thinks he does."

Is that how it went? It was bothering me that the story was blending into real life. I couldn't tell where one ended and the other began. I looked down at the postcard.

"Okay, look. Say Emerson — the real guy — does get hurt in battle. On the island of Saipan, like the magazine says. But instead of dying, he ends up with a doctor, and his face is changed. He looks different."

"But your grandma doesn't know," said Dia, getting into it more and more. "Because how could she? The magazine said he's dead and everyone thinks he is."

"Which is why he sends her this postcard," I said. "She already knows it's got a clue in it, because he told her he used the idea in his stories. She goes to the hotel just like we did, finds the story, and now she knows what happened. She knows that Fang's bad guys kept Nick away from her, and she knows her boyfriend is still alive!"

Dia was quiet for a while. "Except for the fact that we're totally mixing up real life with the story, that sounds about right."

"You think so?"

"I just thought of something," she said. "Your grandma keeps the story hidden in the hotel and doesn't take it with her because her father might find it. I bet that's it. But why do the dates she writes in the margins stop? Did she stop coming to read the story?"

I didn't know. It was too much to keep in my head. I suddenly felt stumped, stopped. "He writes that the story continues in Chapter III. But the postcard only led to the hotel. What if the card is the only clue that survived?"

Dia looked at me. "Let me see it again."

I gave it to her. She flipped it to the back side and grinned. "The postcard had *one* clue for your grannie, but it has *two* for us." She read the card aloud. "Sixteen-thirty Beach Drive Northeast. Sounds like an address to me. What is it?"

"Where she lived, I think," I said. "Her father's house."

Dia's face lit up. "She lived there? With Fang? Is the house still there?"

I shrugged. "I'm not from around these parts."

"The library will tell us," she said. "Let's find the house. That address, Henry, is another clue."

Suddenly, I was tired. This had gone on way too long. "Wait. I have to go to the hospital to see my dad. All I wanted to do was see the hotel. Not get dragged into something that never ends. My dad's expecting me."

"So call him. He's probably asleep, anyway," she said.

"You know they drug people to keep them from pestering the nurses. Besides, don't you want to read Chapter III?"

"There may not even *be* a Chapter III."

"Oh, there's a Chapter III, Bob," she said. "If I know Nicky Falcon, he's going to find his Marnie. And we're going to find out how!"

CHAPTER TWENTY-SEVEN

Why I just followed her, I couldn't tell you, but after three blocks we were at the Mirror Lake Public Library.

"Marnie saw Nick here, in the first chapter," I said. "It's cool that it's still here."

"We go to the best spots," said Dia.

The library was a funky old building on one edge of a park with a lake in the middle. It looked like a Spanish mission and was cool inside, and quiet. A couple of old men were reading newspapers in big chairs, while some were just sitting and staring. A white-haired lady in a sweater the color of pistachio ice cream was unshelving books, peering at their covers over her glasses, and reshelving them.

Dia marched to the reference desk, where a young woman looked up from her computer screen. "Can I help you?" she said.

"We're wondering if this old house is still around," said Dia. She read out the address.

The woman hummed to herself as if she had heard the address before, got up, tugged a box off a nearby shelf, and emptied a stack of brochures on the desk. Her frown evaporated when she found what she was looking for. "I thought so. It's called the Monroe-Davis House. Sometimes known as the Awnings. It's from the early 1900s. It's owned now by the St. Petersburg Historical Society."

"Can people get in to see it?" I asked.

"Wednesday to Saturday, noon to three," she read.

"Noon?" I said. "But, I've got to —"

"That's fine," Dia said to the librarian as she pulled me outside to the steps.

"But it's only ten-thirty," I said. "I can't waste that much time —"

"You won't. I'll show you the Pier. Where Nick wanted to meet Grandma? You gotta see it."

I couldn't believe it, but she started walking, and I followed her. We walked toward the water, went all the way across the blazing hot white bridge to the Pier, limped back, walked along the bay, then turned north into narrow streets paved with dark bricks. It was a real hike, especially in the heat, and we had to stop for water bottles twice, but Dia convinced me it made more sense than finding a bus stop and waiting to make connections. A little over an hour after we'd left the library we were standing under big trees shaggy with Spanish moss at the corner of Beach Drive and 17th Street.

Number 1630 was a big square white house with a red tile roof under the shade of tall, mossy oak trees. A low iron fence circled the yard. Like most houses I'd seen, the yard was fairly small, and the house was close to the street, but it was big. Nearly every window — and there were dozens of them — was shaded by a large white awning trimmed in red. The water breezes kept the awnings inflating with air as if they were breathing.

"The Historical Society," Dia said, reading a sign on the front lawn. "We're visiting Fang's house, T-Bone. We totally lucked out."

T-Bone?

We unlatched the iron gate, paid the student prices with Dia's babysitting money, and joined the first tour of the day.

The guide took us through large over-decorated rooms, saying that much of the furniture and fixtures had been brought in from the hotels that Fang — "Mr. Monroe" — had owned. Along the way, she told us how Patterson Monroe created a railroad empire stretching the whole length of the Gulf coast, that he built this house in 1906, and it was remodeled in the 1920s when his son Quincy inherited the business. The fact that Grandma used to live in the house, actually *lived* there, shocked me when I thought of the tiny box she had died in.

My heart skipped when the guide mentioned my grandmother as we headed into the vast dining room. "Quincy's daughter, Agnes, was ill for many years and lived with a nurse in the bungalow," she said. "It was a place she loved and called her own. Her mother, Ada, died when she was young, and so her father doted on her. Living with her in the bungalow was her favorite tiger-striped kitten, Malkin, whose photo you'll see later on the tour."

Dia grabbed my arm. Again. "Did you hear that, Sandy?"

"Grandma had a kitten named Malkin?" I said.

"No, the bungalow," Dia whispered.

Hearing the word, the guide looked over and said, "That building is not on the tour yet. We're currently renovating it and hope to open it this fall. Right now, the bungalow houses Mr. Monroe's extensive personal library, which is slowly being brought to the big house. To your left is the study used by architect Benjamin Clinton Davis, who bought the house in 1954 after Quincy Monroe and his daughter moved to Europe —"

"Europe? Dad never told me about that —" I whispered to Dia, when she tugged me hard behind one of the columns. "Hey!"

"Shhh!" she said, a glint in her eye. "First of all, are you, like . . . awesomely rich?"

"Me? No way. Did you hear what the lady said —"

"Are you the 'Railroad Prince' or something?"

I had never thought of it that way. But of course I wasn't, since Dad was never acknowledged as part of the Monroe family. "No. No," I whispered. "Besides, Monroe lost everything soon after my dad was born. He lost his fortune a long time ago. That's why Grandma was in a dumpy little house —"

Dia suddenly grew cold. "A dumpy little house? Like mine, you mean."

"Come on, no. I didn't mean that —"

Her hand slapped over my mouth. "Shhh!"

Just before the guide moved to the next room, she looked around as if checking to see that everyone was with her. Dia and I made ourselves thin behind the column. The tour left the room. We were alone.

"Look, I'm sorry," I whispered. "I didn't mean —"

"Just never mind," she snapped.

"Will you stop that?" I said. "You never let me finish a —"

"So you're *not* thinking what I'm thinking?" she said, interrupting me again.

I looked at her. "You want to sneak into the bungalow."

"Where Grandma lived?" she said. "Uh, yeah."

As if Grandma were her grandma.

Again, I just followed her, darting out of the house and across the back lawn.

Darting across the back lawn! Like a criminal!

The little house was separated from the main one by a sidewalk and a hedge. It was a low, stucco building, small and partially hidden by a high bank of wild bushes that fell over it from the edge of the property. It was white like the main house, tile-roofed, and almost perfectly square, with a porch running along the front. We stepped up to it. Wicker furniture stood here and there on the awninged porch as if someone lived there.

It struck me more than once — more than a hundred times! — that I should be at the hospital because in, like, a minute, we would be caught and get arrested and the police would search my backpack and find the postcard and know that it was us snooping at the hotel and my mom would rush down here and take me back and Dad would drink again and fall a second time but Mrs. Keese wouldn't see him and just go on hanging her laundry until it was too late and I'd see his face popping up out of a coffin, but —

Sometimes you just go with it, and I was going with it now.

Sidling up between the bushes on the back side of the bungalow, we cupped our hands and peeked in a window. The inside was scattered with short ladders and buckets and tools and coils of electrical wire. There were also cartons of books and papers just like at Grandma's house, and old furniture under sheets.

"I could totally live here," said Dia.

After first checking to see if any security wires were visible, she began to fiddle with a windowsill, got nowhere, then went around the corner. I peeked toward the house and saw a new tour assembling on the street and heading up the sidewalk. "We have to hurry. Dia —" I didn't see her anywhere.

The back door swung out a pinch, and her face appeared, smiling.

"You coming in?"

CHAPTER TWENTY-EIGHT

It was hot and dark inside the bungalow. Cobwebs hung across the main room. Something alive moved between the walls, which gave me the creeps until I thought of Nick's terrier-sized rat, and I almost didn't mind. Dia went right for the boxes and began to sift through them for signs of anything that looked like a magazine, a manuscript, or a postcard.

I knew it was close to impossible that anything might still be there. But when I saw my great-grandfather's library in dozens of boxes and filling the shelves, it reminded me of Grandma's messy house and all the boxes there and that the whole mystery had started in a place like this.

I set to work right away, too. Or tried to. Among the ghostly furniture I saw what looked like a wheel peeking out from under a dusty sheet. Dust bloomed in the air when I lifted the sheet. It was an ancient wheelchair. The seat and back were made of darkened brown wicker, splitting now, worn in several places, and fraying apart.

"Dia," I said.

She turned from her carton and went quiet. "Wow."

It wasn't the one from Dad's photograph, but maybe an earlier one. It saddened me to think of Grandma going through wheelchairs one after another for so many years. All Dad's stories about doctors and hospitals and Grandma's mysterious accident suddenly became real, and it hurt. It was almost as if she were there in the room with us, sitting in that chair, young again. *What would she say to me?* My throat tightened.

For a while we didn't say much, just emptied boxes quietly, found nothing, and repacked them. I kept thinking how I should be at the hospital and how time was passing, but I kept looking, anyway. Maybe I thought that the better the story I came up with, the less Dad would be mad that it took me so long to visit him. Then Dia went quiet over a carton she had been digging in. When I looked up, her hand flicked out of the box, holding a postcard.

"My God, Corey," she said.

The card was dated 1949 and was from a place called Al Lang Field, which Dia said was a baseball diamond near the Pier. It was addressed to Beach Drive, but bore no message or inscribed chapter number. When we held it up to the light, we saw no pinhole anywhere.

"Keep digging," she said. "I *will* score on this, Fergus. You better believe I will."

We found two more postcards over the next half hour. One from 1948 featured a guy named Webb and his huge drug store called Webb City. The third was of a place called The Fountain of Youth and was dated 1950. Again, none of them had a message or a pinhole.

"So why no clues on these?" Dia asked, slumping into the wheelchair with the postcards on her lap.

"I —"

"I'll tell you why," she said. "Nick sent the cards to

Marnie to show he was going to be there. He was still trying to see her."

"Emerson," I corrected. "Sent to my grandmother —"

"He was trying to see her," she said, ignoring me, "but she never made it to any of these places."

"Maybe. We don't know."

"I do. He was trying, but her father wouldn't let her go. He's Fang, remember? He had no soul. And as much as Marnie loved Nick, Fang hated him. I bet she never even saw these postcards. That's why they're sitting here with Fang's stuff and not with hers at your house."

I glanced up at her, sunlight in my face. "You have this all figured out, don't you?"

Even in the dark, I saw her do a grinny thing with her eyebrows, then her expression changed. She went kind of, I don't know, *soft.*

"You . . . ," she whispered, ". . . the sun . . . you're . . ." Slowly, she leaned forward in the wheelchair, across the slanting light, and reached toward me as if she was going to touch my hair. For some reason, I just watched her face get closer to mine. I didn't move.

"Move!" she said. She pushed me out of the way, the

195

chair rolled back, and she grabbed something from the shelf behind me.

It flashed in the sunlight coming in the window.

"Holy crikey!" she gasped.

It was a silver cigarette case studded with a blue stone.

CHAPTER TWENTY-NINE

Dia's fingers trembled in the streaked darkness of the bungalow as she turned the cigarette case over and over. "Nick sees Fang open this in the hotel. When he first sees Marnie."

She opened it now, and the smell of stale tobacco blossomed from inside. Folded neatly behind a few ancient cigarettes was . . . a postcard.

"Oh, whoa and a half," she said, her mouth hanging open. She handed the case to me. "You do it."

My hands were like an old man's again, shaking and

cold. I slipped the postcard out from behind the cigarettes and unfolded it.

The front had a picture of a tall but obviously fake waterfall. The rocks that formed it were partly real and partly cement molded to look like rocks. Water splashed down from level to level and finally into a flowery pond at the bottom. The whole waterfall was surrounded by vines and dangling branches. Over the top of the picture it read, "Beautiful Sunken Gardens."

I turned the card over. It was addressed to Beach Drive and postmarked from St. Petersburg on May 14, 1952.

"It was 1944 when they first met," I said. "Eight years have passed. Eight years. I guess he still liked her."

"Of course he still liked her," said Dia. "Quit stalling."

Moving my fingers over the card, I felt three lines stamped inklessly into the message area:

III

"Uh-huh, uh-huh," said Dia, "and is there a hole in it? My gosh, Willy, will you hold it up to the light?"

I don't know why I was taking so long. Maybe I didn't want to be disappointed. Maybe I just wanted it to last longer.

When I finally moved the card up into the window, my heart nearly stopped. Near the top of the card, just under the top ledge of the waterfall, was a tiny twinkle of light. "Oh, whoa . . ."

Dia snatched the card away and looked at it. "Holy, Buster!" she cried. "She never saw this one. He was hiding it from her. We are *so* lucky. A lot of the old tourist places are long gone. Nothing but dust. My dad could list them for you. He's always going on about old Florida junk vanishing and stuff. That's why he always drives over the Gandy. He loves that bridge. Gandy-Gandy-Gandy —"

"Dia!" I said, putting the cigarette case back on the shelf. "The point?"

"The point is, not Sunken Gardens. It's still around. In fact, it's not even that far away. Johnny, this is it. Chapter III. We are so close I can almost smell the recycled water." A smile lit up her whole bronze face. She looked so . . . so . . . jeez, never mind!

"Your grandma never saw this card, I know it," she said, slipping out the door, and flipping the latch to lock behind us. "Fang hid it from her and kept it. He probably knew it meant something, but not what. And supposing he never figured it out, whatever is hidden in the waterfall might still be there. Chapter III? Oh, yeah. Buff up your reading glasses, Elmer —"

"Dia, wait. Fifty-plus years in a public place? With probably ten million people all over it. And storms and hurricanes . . . ?"

There was something in the smile she was making now as we moved across the lawn to the gate that told me she had stopped listening to me and was already thinking about our route to Sunken Gardens.

I sighed. "So are we going there right now?"

"Tommy Boy, we are *so* going there! Only not right now. I gotta eat really bad. Plus you can meet my mom!"

CHAPTER THIRTY

Not that I was surprised, but Dia's house was so fast and strange, that from the moment we got off the bus, ran across her yard, and stepped through the door, I felt as if I were falling.

Her mother was a heavy block of a lady with big hair who laughed the whole time we were there. She was laughing when we reached the screen door. She was laughing when we opened it. She laughed when Dia barged in.

"Deeeeee-aaaa!" she howled. Her greeting was like a song. "You must have smelled your favorite —"

Dia peeked over her mother's shoulder (not difficult, because Mrs. Martin was so short). "Mmm, meat loaf!"

"And beans!" her mother laughed. "And malangas!" Her hands were covered in red ground meat. She raised them from the pan on the counter. "Here, here, smooch!"

"Mom, how long for supper?" Dia asked. "Oh, this is Kenny. His dad fell off a ladder and he's staying with his neighbor. He's Mrs. Huff's grandson."

"Jason," I said.

"Ooh," Mrs. Martin came at me and squeezed my face between her wrists. "I'm sorry about your grandma," she said, smiling sadly. "She was lovely to my Dia. You poor boy."

"Thank you," I said.

She kissed me, then pulled back and frowned. "Dee-Dee! I hope you two haven't been —"

"Mom!" she screamed.

"— smoking," said her mother. "I smell cigarettes!"

"Gosh, Mom, no," said Dia. "It's Tim's postcard. It stinks."

Her mother laughed as if she'd known all along, not even looking at the postcard, but turning back to the oven. "That's fine. Forty-five minutes. Have some bread if you're hungry. Sit at the table. Eat the table, if you're that hungry. Ha! Kevin, sit."

"Jason," I said.

"Can't, Mom," said Dia, heading back toward one of the bedrooms. "Gotta get on the Internet. Dad coming?"

"He called. The Gandy's stuffed up like a nose. But not too long."

The Gandy. Again.

Dia sighed. "Why does Dad go that way?"

Mrs. Martin snickered. "He's your father, that's why."

Dia darted back across the kitchen, stuck her face into the refrigerator, pulled out a plastic bag of sliced cheese, shoved a slice into her mouth, gave me two of my own, and was down the hall to her room in less than a minute. The layout of the house was pretty much like my grandma's except that the garage and the bedrooms were on the opposite sides of the house.

Dia stopped abruptly, nearly knocking me down, and started back toward the kitchen. "Mom, can you or Dad take us to Sunken Gardens before it closes?" she called over my shoulder.

"He can. I need to watch this, okay?"

"Okay."

As we left the kitchen a third time, Dia spun on her heels, slid into the bathroom, and slammed the door in my face.

"Start the computer," she said through the door.

"What?" shouted her mother from the kitchen.

"NOTHING!" yelled Dia.

"Okay!" said her mother.

Holy crow! I checked both bedrooms for the smaller bed, found it, slumped into her desk chair, and started her computer.

While I sat there exhausted by a minute's worth of loud talk, I glanced around her room. It was small, like the one I had in my grandmother's house. There were pillows everywhere on the floor, books stuffed into built-in shelves along the wall under the window, a dresser piled with more books and makeup stuff, and a pair of dolls curled up on her bed as if they were napping. A police car drove past on the street outside her window. I knew it wasn't after us. It wasn't even driving slow; and for sure it wasn't the same officer as at the hotel. But I had this idea that if someone were looking down on me lately, it wouldn't have looked good.

Lying to the police at the hospital, sneaking into an

abandoned hotel, breaking into a Historical Society site? And who was that in the hotel, anyway? Who was . . . the Limper? Who made that strange call to my house? The same guy? A different guy? Could people really be following me? Did they want to stop me from finding the story? Was it bigger than that? What did they not want me to know about? *Was I finding things I shouldn't find?*

That made my neck tingle. My eyelids began to twitch. What had I gotten myself into? Should I tell Mom everything —

Oh, my gosh! Dad! I looked at my watch. It had somehow gotten to be late afternoon. How the heck did that happen? I pulled out my phone and called the hospital right away. After being transfered a few times, I got his nurse.

"He's sleeping," she said. "He was asking about you. Can I tell him you're coming?"

"Yes, yes. I've been busy with the house packing all day." She said nothing.

"So, yes. I'll be there soon."

"I'll tell him." She hung up. I so had to get there.

Not hearing a flush from the bathroom yet — it was that close — I made a quick call to Hector.

"Dude!" he said when he heard my voice. "I'm dying here! Rain and hammocks don't mix. And by that I mean it's raining. When are you coming home? I mean, how's your dad, but when are you coming home?"

"I don't know," I said.

"What?" yelled Mrs. Martin.

"What *what*?" called Dia from the bathroom.

"NOTHING!" I shouted back.

"Okay!" they chimed together.

"Hector, look," I whispered into the phone, "there's a kind of mystery I found. At least I think it's a mystery." I told him as much as I could remember.

"Your dad's lawyer friend, Mr. Fracker, died sixty years ago? So who was the guy using his name? No kidding a bizarre mystery. A bizarre zombie mystery. Singapore? The Everglades? Do people actually escape from alligators?"

"It's a story," I told him. "So maybe. I don't know. That's the least of it. There's so much nutty stuff. I feel as if I'm drowning in it."

"What was that weird word?" he asked.

"Oobarab."

"Sounds like a kind of animal."

"You're thinking of caribou or baboon or something."
I spelled it for him, then heard the bathroom door finally open. "Gotta go. We'll talk soon."

Dia came in and saw me with my phone. "Did you call Mrs. K to tell her you're eating here?"

Gosh! "Good idea," I said. So I called to tell her I'd see her later. She said, "I'll hide my key in the mailbox for you. And see? It was good to put on lights, wasn't it?"

"You were right," I said.

When I hung up, Dia was reading the home page of Sunken Gardens. We scanned through the slideshow of historical pictures, the onscreen map, and finally the virtual tour, none of which were all that helpful. We couldn't find where the waterfall in the postcard might have been or whether it was still there.

"This doesn't mean anything," she said. "It could still be there."

"Except that don't they tear everything down here?" I said.

She turned. I thought she was going to say something to me. Instead, she yelled into my face. "MOM, WE REALLY HAVE TO GO TO SUNKEN GARDENS! WHERE'S DAD?"

I nearly fell out of my chair. "What the —"

Her mother appeared, laughing, at the door of Dia's room, wiping her hands on a towel. "S'okay with your neighbor you go there, Jimmy? And then you eat here after?"

"Oh, yes," I said. "She's fine with it."

Mrs. Martin smiled. "Then, you better move it! Your dad's here!"

"My dad?" I said.

Dia got up. "No, mine, Spinky."

A skinny man with a full head of black hair as wild as Mrs. Martin's came into the room, grabbed Dia, and whirled her around. One of her sneakers flew off. "Poppy!" she yelled.

"Dee-ey!" he said. "And who's this?"

"You know. The boy on the bus," said Dia.

I shook his hand. "Jason. I think," I said.

"Nice to meet you. Staying for supper?"

"We need a ride to Sunken Gardens first, then we'll eat," said Dia. She spun around at me, and frowned. "So, your toes glued to the floor or what?"

Both Martin parents laughed and laughed. I guessed they must have had a lot of fun with Dia saying crazy things all the time. The next thing I heard was the jangle of car keys and we were out the door. The three of us piled in Mr. Martin's front seat because the back was filled with all kinds of stuff.

For the next fifteen minutes, he talked nonstop. He had grown up in Cuba but moved to Tampa with his parents when he was young. They had worked in a place called Ybor City, where the big cigar-making business was. He moved to St. Petersburg when he and Mrs. Martin got married, but they have dinner with his folks in Tampa every week.

"I *love* Sunken Gardens!" he said. "It opened a hundred years ago, and it's sunken because it's in a sinkhole, I bet you didn't know. It almost went under a few times, but keeps coming back better than ever. I love all the old places that are still around." He reached over my head to the back seat and plopped an old cigar box in my lap.

"No thanks," I said. "I don't —"

"Ooh, Daddy," Dia said, flipping the box open. Inside were maps and brochures for attractions all over Florida. Places called Sulphur Springs, Paradise Park, Orchid Jungle, Gatorama. Some of the places, he said, didn't exist anymore.

Dia and I fished around until we found one from Sunken Gardens from the 1960s. I got excited to think that the waterfall might actually still be there.

"Take the map. It could be handy," Mr. Martin said as we drove into the parking lot of the Gardens.

"You bet," said Dia. "We're solving a mystery, Dad."

He laughed. "That's my Dia. Here's a twenty. Be safe?"

"Always!"

The sun was starting to dip, but it was still hot. We had less than an hour and a half before closing time. Dia gave her father a hug, then grabbed my hand and pulled me toward the entrance.

"See you back out here at six," her father said. "I'll be parked outside the gift shop."

"He's cool," I said.

"Yeah, he is. Hurry up."

S.83—Alligators in Tropical Florida
Sarasota Jungle Gardens   3C-H959

CHAPTER THIRTY-ONE

Ten minutes and sixteen dollars later, Dia and I were inside Sunken Gardens. They might have called it Sunken Jungle. It was thick with high trees and low tropical plants and overflowed with flowers and vines and blossoming bushes that spilled over onto narrow winding paths. Ponds and marshes dotted the sides of the paths while a green stream slithered through the whole park like a snake.

We found a bench in the Oak Pavilion, a brick patio surrounded by tall trees, and spread her dad's old map and a new one on our knees. The garden was as hot as a sauna;

the air was close, thick, and hard to breathe. Birds cackled and screamed from somewhere just beyond us.

"It's changed, but not that much," said Dia. "Which is good."

Mothers with strollers went by. Grandparents and grandchildren. An older woman all dressed in pink and yellow passed our bench, smiling. Next came three workers, one carrying a short ladder, another a rolled-up hose, laughing at something one just said. Everyone seemed so much fresher than me. I was soaked.

"There are only two waterfalls on the map," said Dia finally. "We have to follow the paths nearly all the way to the back."

The moment we got up, I saw a flash of shiny black suit vanish among the plants. *Are you kidding me? No way. I'm seeing things.*

I hurried after Dia. We wormed our way down one path, where we saw giant bird cages with — what else? — parrots in them. I couldn't help thinking about the little connections — the cut-through, the flower shop, the Gandy Bridge, the parrots. I felt as if the story were going on around us. We passed the old fenced-in entrance building that was no longer used and some flamingos lolling next to a pond. There was rustle behind me. Turning, I saw a beret disappearing behind the building, and I knew for certain.

"They're here!" I whispered. "Dia, we're being followed. I'm seeing people from the funeral home."

She smiled. "You see dead people?"

"I'm serious."

She glanced down the path herself now, her smile fading. "You know what? I'd be more surprised if you didn't see them. It means we're onto something. Keep moving."

Besides my being nervous as we hurried on, I found the paths very confusing. We went over some of them twice, wasting time we didn't have, and dead-ended in an open garden that took us all the way back to the entrance. I could barely follow the new map and hoped that Dia could make sense of her father's old one. When we finally heard rushing water, I got excited. But it was a small waterfall, not at all the one on the card.

I was disappointed. Disappointed and angry that I had spent the whole day with Dia when I was supposed to be seeing my father. Besides, were we being followed? Actually *followed*? This was serious, wasn't it?

I stopped. "Forget this," I said.

"What?"

"The whole thing. What are we doing here? I don't care if there's a mystery. What difference does it make? My dad's in the hospital, for crying out loud. I should be there! Can we just go —"

Dia looked me in the eyes. "Hold on. Is this how you deal with everything? Just quit?"

"What are you talking about?"

"Stop mowing the lawn. Stop thinking about Grandma. You're like the guys tearing down that old hotel because it's not new enough. Jeez. Have some guts, will you? We only have a little over a half hour left. If there's any chance of finding out about Nick and Marnie, we have to. Marnie's your *grandmother,* after all."

"But who says we'll even find anything?" I said. "It's probably long gone —"

"You're gone," she snapped. "I'm going searching."

She stormed off, and the parrots cackled behind me. She made me feel I don't know what, but she had one thing right, and it hit home. Marnie *was* my grandmother. If there was anything to discover about her, I guessed I could spend a half hour finding out what it was. I followed the girl.

We hustled down all the paths, keeping clear of people as best we could. I was sure we were still passing places we had just seen — we saw the workers and the smiling lady three more times — but it was all so green and hot and thick I couldn't even be sure. By this time, security guards were moving more obviously down the paths, urging people gently back toward the main entrance. A guard came our way. I pretended to wait, smiling, while Dia leaned over and fiddled with her sneakers.

"The Gardens are closing," I said to her.

"Coming, honey," she said brightly. When the guard passed, she did an about face and plunged into the over-growth behind us.

"'Honey'?" I said. "What the — *ooof!*"

She yanked me into the bushes after her. "Shush up!" she hissed. Crouching, she glanced both ways, then turned again and darted under some hangy things to a back part of the path.

She stopped. "Holy cow!"

We faced a very tall waterfall made mostly of concrete molded to look like rock. The greenery was different. Vines hung from higher trees than were there before, and the bushes surrounding the waterfall were bigger in some cases and smaller in others, but it was the same waterfall on the postcard.

"Amazing!" I said.

The postcard's pinhole was directly in the bottom side of the uppermost ledge about seven feet up from the ground. Water gushed out of a pipe up top and tumbled down several ledges to a pool at the bottom.

"There must be plumbing for the waterfall, which means pipes and stuff hidden near the top," she said, squinting toward the upper ledges. "I say there's a hatch somewhere up there that hides the waterworks. How do you want to do this?"

I thought about boosting her up, then about her boosting me up, which might have worked better, or about finding a log or thick stick and both of us grabbing it and poking at the ledge —

"Time's up. Get in the pond and lean over," she said. "I'm going to stand on your back."

"What am I?" I said. "A cheerleader —"

"In and lean," she snapped. "Do it. It!"

Looking both ways, I slid off my shoes and stepped into the pond. The water was cool and wasn't deep. She got in after me and pushed hard against my back. "Down!" I nearly fell, then steadied myself, standing there like a tipped-over "L," while she jumped on my back piggyback style. Then, she slowly got to her feet.

"Stop wobbling!"

"I'm standing in muck —," I said.

I couldn't see her, but I could feel her leaning and reaching upward, when out of nowhere goldfish, huge ones, began to slither around my ankles.

Oh man. I closed my eyes. She pulled one foot away from me and planted it on a ledge halfway up the waterfall.

"I see the plumbing box under the top ledge," she said. "I knew it!" She tested her footing to bring the other leg up, then slipped back. I half caught her in my arms.

"Watch the hands, Romeo!" she said.

"Sorry."

She hoisted herself on my back again, then perched as high as possible on the fake rocks, one foot on my spine, water sloshing over her hands and arms. She began jostling and banging the hatch until it suddenly swung open. She rooted around for a few seconds when something heavy and square fell out from among the pipes and dials and wires under the ledge. It tumbled down the rocks past her, barely missing my head, and splashed at my feet. It was a shallow metal box just like the first.

"We have it!" she cried. She reached up once more to snap the plumbing hatch closed, then hopped down next to me. Meanwhile, the box had fallen open in the water, and papers had spilled out. They started to sink under the pond water.

"Get the pages!" she said. I grabbed them from the water and wiped the pages on my jeans until I saw I was smearing the type.

"Good one, Smitty!" she said. "Quit it —"

SNAP! A branch cracked.

We froze.

"Uh-oh . . . ," she whispered.

We stood there, dripping wet, our hands full of soggy paper, while someone rustled in the bushes beyond the end of the path.

4A-H806

CHAPTER THIRTY-TWO

"Security!" I hissed.

Dia listened, then shook her head. "No. Security is minimum wage. They'd be running up the path before slogging though the mud. Only criminals like us do that."

"How do you know that stuff?" I said. "I mean, how do you even know to *say* stuff like that?"

She shrugged. "I say everything."

"Yeah, I know!"

"So, come on," she said. "If it is the Side Order of Oobarab, I don't want to end up on the wrong side of a car trunk. Even if you're in there with me. Move it!"

The bushes crashed noisily behind us now. Something scraped and then clicked like metal on the sidewalk. Was someone dragging a huge gun? The sound fell behind as we raced toward the entrance.

"Hey! Skvirt!" yelled a voice.

"Oh my gosh!" I choked. "It's the German dagger thrower!"

Snapping and footsteps came from two directions now. Then a third set of steps rushed along the path behind us. It sounded like women's heels.

"Holy crud!" Dia swore. "This is serious!"

We dashed away under overhanging palm branches and into a dirt area between two sections of the winding path.

"Now where?" I huffed.

"Up there!" she said. Stuffing both maps into her cutoffs, she jumped up the side of a tree. Right left, right left, she climbed up. I followed her. The sounds passed beneath us. We couldn't see who it was. We heard more footsteps and more scraping on the paths nearby, but saw no one then, either.

It finally got quiet below. We jumped to the ground.

"Straight along the back and over the wall," said Dia.

"But the front gate is still open," I said.

"Where do you think the Oobarabs will be waiting? They've followed us everywhere. We can't make it easy for them. Over the wall to the block behind the Gardens. This way."

We ran through the palm bushes and were over the wall and on the back street before anyone saw us. We went to a corner a block down then circled around behind the gift shop to the main street, where Dia waved to her father to come over. I sorted the pages. There were ten, altogether. Mr. Martin drove up a minute later, laughing as before. He handed us some half-melted Italian ices. "Don't tell Mommy about these. Have fun?"

"The best, Dad," said Dia, climbing in the front with me. Then, setting the soggy pages across our kness, she whispered: "Doogie, prepare to read Chapter III."

Right there on the way to her house for meat loaf and malangas (whatever they were), we began to read.

CHAPTER THIRTY-THREE

— III —

THE HUNTED MAN

By Emerson Beale

My last day in Singapore was one of falling flowers and cackling birds. I left Harrow's place by the rickety back stairs, hoping they wouldn't buckle under me before I got to solid ground. I ducked into an alley seconds before the dead man's family arrived. They looked like they wanted to talk with their fists, then let machetes drive their points home. I wished my friend well.

"One question," I said before we parted.

"Shoot. Well, don't *shoot*..."

"Why did you help me, after all?" I asked him. "I'm nobody to you."

Harrow looked beyond the buildings to the single tree in the neighborhood that hadn't been blighted by the war. It was pink with early blossoms that spun around in the breeze. The smile on his face seemed sad. "You're nobody to me, true, but even a nobody sometimes has a heart. I fancy I know what's in yours. Or, rather, *who*'s in yours." His little laugh then was full of hurt. "I had a Marnie once. I lost her. Don't lose yours."

Then he said he'd probably never see me again. I hoped he was wrong. He headed for the airport. I headed for the dock by way of the post office. I figured if everything went right, I'd be back in Florida before the big brown envelope was. I also figured that not everything would go right.

My timing was perfect. A beat-up old tub of a tanker out of San Diego named *Coronado* was loading for departure. I thanked Harrow silently for the tip.

I hadn't been there more than three minutes, sizing up my chances of getting onboard, when I heard the rattling cough of something iron, and the blue sedan rolled across the dock and heaved to a stop. Maybe I was still delirious or maybe I didn't have time to wonder how in hell that car ever got to Singapore, but its doors squealed open and who else but Skull slunk out of the cab, socks first.

Two and a half years had done nothing for his complexion. He was as faded as hotel sheets. When he snapped his fingers, Tall Man unfolded himself from the sedan's backseat.

No sooner had they begun arguing with some locals and searching the crowds than a handful of toughs from the alley swaggered in. The local chapter of the Oobarab Society was anxious to make a name for itself. Skull began to point, and the goons deployed across the dock. When he slapped his shoulder three times, his parrot fluttered out of the car and settled on him. But he had a new addition to his menagerie now.

"Bring it!" he called.

The giant clicked open the trunk, tugged once, then again, and a tiger, all ten rippling feet of it, slithered foot by foot by foot by foot down onto the dock.

"Malkin, heel!" Skull said.

Dia and I looked at each other. *Malkin? The kitten?*

When the tiger shook its massive head, the thugs' fedoras nearly blew away. Malkin then poured itself over the dock to Skull, who took hold of the leash with both hands. It was a thick silver chain studded with blue stones.

Was it just my aching temples? Had my brain been blasted by that explosion. Or was this getting a little crazy now? Maybe it was all three.

I watched Skull pull something out of his coat pocket. It was a rag of blood-stained khaki. He dangled it under the tiger's nose. Malkin sniffed it, pulled away, and lolled its massive head from side to side.

I hugged the backside of a shipping container. There came a low rumbling sound, then the shoosh of soft tires along the dock. The rumbling stopped. Peering around the container, I saw a motorcycle and sidecar. Driving it was a vision in purple wearing goggles and a veil. In its sidecar was Redbeard. He popped out. "Madame, vait," he said.

His hands plunged deep in his cloak, the German rolled over to Mr. Bone, fuming.

"Ve gonna get him zis time, Shkull, eh?" he muttered. "Kuz if we not, Fank be real enkry."

Corpse-face glared down at the short German. "Hoping so is what you oughta do, Punch. The Order won't like him slipping through the claws of us. Malkin, sniff!"

Roused, the tiger pawed steadily down the dock

toward the ship's plank, jerking Skull forward as if he were a marionette on hooch. Malkin's growl was not quite as loud as the ship's engines, just low and deep and threatening enough to turn my vertebrae to jelly. Skull and his striped pet looked as if they were setting up shop and would be there awhile.

What could I do? I couldn't go back into town. The crowd of well-wishers at Harrow's hotel would have doubled by now and would be combing the streets. I had to get on that ship. More than that, I needed to know whether my wounds and Harrow's work on them had done anything more than hurt like heck.

So I went up to him.

I went right up to Skull, to see if he knew me.

The bird on his shoulder had eyed me in a crazed way from the moment I'd emerged from behind the container, and cawed maniacally as I approached, *"Paaaaangg!"* The tiger sniffed me up and down, thumping its paws heavily on my shoes.

"Malkin, off!" Skull growled, yanking the animal's chain harder than I would have.

Quivering inside my clothes, I patted my pockets, pretending to search for a cigarette. "Say, pal. Gotta smoke?" I was surprised that even my voice sounded different in the open air. Lower. Gruffer.

"Scram off, kid," the ugly man growled, scanning my face for no more than a moment. "I'm working here."

He pushed past me and walked on. It hurt to smile, but I managed it. "No problem. I was thinking of quitting, anyway."

Still trembling, I went to the plank.

The ship's purser stopped me at the bottom. In his forties, weathered, stocky, his eyes mechanical under a brimmed cap, he stood blocking the plank. The gray waters of the South China Sea seemed endless behind him. I thought of the black endless Gulf and Marnie on the other side of it and ached to see her. Marnie, Marnie, Marnie.

"You got fare and papers?" the purser asked me.

"I got," I said, taking a small wad of bills from my pocket. I told you Harrow was an ace guy. The best.

The man squinted at my face, then at the money, then at the documents I handed him. A shiver ran up my spine to my neck. I glanced to my left. Only the water, gray and flat. To my right, Skull, Mr. Tall, the German, the tiger, the parrot, and half the Malay branch of the Order. The man folded the bills into his breast pocket and handed back the documents. He nodded at me slowly, knowingly, wrinkling up his forehead as he saluted and stepped aside.

"God bless ya, Private Randall Frederick Fracker.
Welcome home."

"Oh my gosh!" I said. "Fracker! The lawyer! Emerson became Fracker! Holy crud — I mean, excuse me! — but I have to tell my dad —"

"Wait! What the heck just happened here?" said Dia. She read the page again. Then a third time.

My brain was popping and stuttering like the engine of that blue sedan. I tried to sort it out for both of us. "Okay, look . . . Emerson Beale . . . I mean, Nick Falcon, was wounded. His face was messed up. Harrow fixed him up, and he looked different. So he came back as Fred Fracker, his dead Army friend. He had his dog tags. He had his papers. Fracker was alone in the world, remember? So Nick used the stuff because his face was so changed. And Nick Falcon became the lawyer that my dad knew years ago —"

"But is that true?" asked Dia. "Because what about the kitten? Malkin is now a *tiger*? And the purple lady? And how does the blue car get all the way to Singapore?"

"I don't know," I said. "I don't know."

"That sounds like some story," said Mr. Martin, slow-ing and pulling into a gas station. "I need to fill up. Five minutes."

He popped out of the car and trotted to the office.

We kept reading.

Teetering for an instant, I saluted the purser back then walked slowly up the plank and onto the deck. When the ship pulled away from Bonehead, his tiger, and the rest of the gang, I realized I had done it. For the moment, I had become someone else. I had slipped past the long arm of Oobarab and was that much closer to home.

Home! I could almost taste it. But my appetite had to wait. Florida was still ten thousand miles away.

After making every stop from Java to Pitcairn, the *Coronado* docked in San Diego two months later. I made friends with the postman and trusted him to do his job. For the next five months I worked my way to Phoenix, Galveston, New Orleans, and Hattiesburg. I caught wind of the Order prowling those places, but they were looking for Nick Falcon, not Freddie Fracker, so I moved on.

Working as an apple picker in Valdosta landed me in a hospital for over half a year with a bout of the malaria I'd contracted in the jungle. The doctor said my heart would suffer from its chronic recurrence. I wished him well, too. Finally, I hit Pensacola, where I was picked up on the southern route by a cigar salesman. He was motoring back to Tampa after three weeks on the road and asked me if I wanted a lift.

He filled me in. First about his wife and seven kids. Then Truman. The Marshall Plan. Stalin. War babies. The latest real estate boom. I told him next to nothing.

"A talker you're not," he said. "But good luck to ya."

He finally dumped me at Charlie Doyle's place. It was a little old Spanish house on 52nd South. You could practically taste the seawater, it was that close to Boca Ciega. Midnight came under a blue-black sky dotted with twinkling stars. I waited an hour more. Two. Making sure everyone everywhere was asleep, I hammered on his door.

Blinking, Doyle answered. He was shirtless in pajama bottoms. "Buddy," he growled at me, "you're two feet away, but I guess they don't make watches where you are. It's half past nothing here. Go away."

I didn't go away.

"It's the middle of the night, pal," he said. "You in a different time zone, or what?"

"It's me," I told him. "Nick Falcon."

His face went suspicous, then sullen. "Nick Falcon is dead. He died on Saipan; everybody knows that. Beat it." He started to turn.

"I sent you an envelope from Singapore over a year ago. If you never got it, I'll have a word with the mailman—"

He swung his face back at mine and examined me for what seemed like forever before his scowl vanished. "You...you...Nick!" He practically leaped from the doorway, wrapped his skinny arms around me, and dragged me in off the street, practically sobbing.

Before I knew it I was sitting in his Florida room, my hands wrapped around a tall glass of anesthesia.

I told him nearly everything. He gaped, cried, whistled, laughed, and finally told me as much as he knew of what had been happening back home.

"I delivered the envelope like you wanted me to. Got myself in the hotel on a repair job and hid it behind the air grate like you asked, but then what? That was, I don't know, fifteen months ago. Then nothing."

"I had to cross ten thousand miles first. My malaria paid me a return visit, too," I said, tapping my chest. "It never goes away for good."

He took that opportunity to refill my prescription, and I told him the rest.

"Dang, Nick. The Secret Order of Oobarab," he said with a low whistle. "Quentin Blaine's underworld army. So they're in Singapore, too? Fang's a scary one, Nick. Or should I say...Freddie? Land is one of his two unholy obessions. He had an eye as dark as swamp water and teeth like a serpent when you saw him last. But it's worse now. You don't want to mess with him lately."

"Way too late for that."

"Golly, Nick. You picked a dangerous girl to fall in love with. She's his other obsession."

I shrugged. "You talk a blue streak. I imagine Marnie has her own mind."

"Maybe," he said. "Look. I didn't read what you had me hide in the hotel, but how the heck would Marnie ever know about it? Like everyone else, she's gotta think you died in Japan four years ago."

I smiled at that. "Not so much. I sent her a postcard when I reached the States."

"A postcard?" Charlie laughed. "You old snooker! That's my idea! I used postcards as a clue while you were still sharpening pencils in grade school!"

I raised my glass to him. "To a writer who shares."

"So you practice what I preach. Does the Order know you're back in Florida?"

"Maybe," I said, stroking my damaged cheek, "but not what I look like."

He nodded. "I remember the date it hit the papers. June twenty-fourth, 1944. I remember because the paper was free that day. First time in three years. It rained all day."

"I have to see her."

"Sure, sure," he said, shaking his head. "I guess I knew that was coming from the first." He turned to the window, looked sadly into the coming dawn, then back at me. "She's...changed, you know."

I felt my heart skip a beat. "Not married?"

"No, no, no. Nothing like that. I guess she still holds a torch for you. No, it's...there was an accident."

"What kind of accident?"

"Nick, she's in a chair. Been there since, I don't know, awhile after I got your envelope. Half a year. Longer."

Hearing it was like dying. Each word was a dagger in my heart. *She's in a chair.* Marnie, my Marnie. I turned away. "It isn't so."

He leaned forward and spoke softly, painfully. "Freakish thing. Flying accident. Fang and Marnie in his danged autogyro. The official story goes he had engine trouble and plunged into the Bay," he said. "He escaped minus an eye. Nick, it crashed hard. Lots of witnesses. She flew out, hit the water. Something about her spine. She was under the water a long time, too.

That messed with her lungs...at the very least. Sorry, Nick. You gotta know the worst."

I heard the words. I couldn't believe them. My heart did. I started blubbering.

"Nicky, look. Fang — he went nuts about it. Blamed himself. He's gone 'off,' they say. He's wrapped the Order around her so tight nobody sees her anymore. They make hugger-mugger midnight trips to clinics. Not just here. Europe, Asia, too. As tough as it was to see her before, it's impossible now. She lives a captive in his compound, if you call it living. She's in that dark castle he calls the Towers."

"I know the place," I said. The image of prison grounds came to me. A prison with Marnie locked inside.

"Nick, a small army patrols the grounds. No phone. No friends. Just doctors, surgeons. You couldn't get to her if you wanted to."

"It's far beyond wanting to," I told him.

He looked at me for a long time. "All right," he said finally. "I'll help you. It won't be easy, but what are friends for? I'll snoop around. Heck, maybe I'll even find out something. Golly, I still can't believe you're here. You escaped. You made it back!" He was near to crying now.

"I'll need better papers," I said.

"Sure, sure. Jeanette will help," he said, wiping his face with his bare arm. "She always loved you. You're staying here, by the way. I'll make up the extra bed. Nick, we need to celebrate. In secret, of course."

I smiled. "Later. First, can I use your typewriter?"

He grinned now. "Still the same old Nick, no matter what you look like. You got some story, I bet."

"Not for the magazine, though. Not yet. And I'll need some postcards."

"Sure. If the post office is still doing its job, she'll know about you."

"Thanks." Doyle had been my friend since I wrote my first mystery. He'd be my friend until my last.

My new identity kept me able to move around without Oobarab on my tail, but Doyle was right. There was no getting close to Fang's tower-topped castle of black stone. It was crawling with thugs. The place was tighter than a drunk on payday.

The one chance I saw was that when the gossip press got a bit too hot about not seeing her, Marnie went out on carefully controlled occasions with a small battalion of nurses. But even that didn't work. For the next eight months, I sent her postcards, visited tourist spots all over town, took them in alone, and came home alone.

As much as he could, Doyle went out, mostly at night, and scouted and searched and scrounged. He'd even taken to wearing all black, from crepe-soled shoes to a slouchy black beret. Month after month passed, and I tapped away, writing it all down.

"Black beret!" I said. "My gosh, it's the same guy! I saw him. We both saw him at Brent's Funeral Home!"

Dia nodded over and over. "And the postcards Nick sent were the ones we found at the bungalow. The ball-field, Webb's drug store. This is so unbelievably cool!"

"Okay, okay," I said, "but wait. Is the Towers the same as the Awnings? It's like the kitten becoming a tiger. That can't be real."

"I don't know," she said. "But maybe it doesn't matter. Does it matter?"

The car slowed and Mr. Martin pulled into their driveway. We took a break while the meat loaf made its way around the table and we talked about things. I told them about my father being Mr. Fixit with the house, skipping the little bit about why he fell from the ladder, and something about Mom traveling from place to place like a Ping-Pong ball. It did the trick. They frowned, then they laughed.

After supper, Mrs. Martin had a class to go to, so she left first, then Dia and I helped her father clean up. When we were finished, I followed her to her room. We sat on her floor pillows and kept on reading and didn't stop until the end.

My new face had bought me time to scout and plan, but I knew that sooner or later I'd have to break cover. It turned out to be later. The web Fang had woven around Marnie was as impenetrable as a Chinese wall. When she was hauled off to some secluded clinic, the trail went cold altogether, as if she no longer existed. I could do nothing but wait for her to surface again. It finally happened in the spring of 1952, four years after my return. Four interminable years.

"Next month Blaine's going to transport his fatness to the capital at Tallahassee," Doyle told me one morning as I peeled myself off a cot soaked with sweat. "Bigwigs from all over. Swindling land from the poor unwashed, I suppose. The usual. He'll be there three or four days."

"Tallahassee," I said, remembering my father and the real estate battle so long ago. It had hurt a lot of people, as it turned out, my father among the rest. "And the Order?"

He wagged his head. "There are more of them guarding Marnie than the Japanese did Saipan. With some new recruits, I hear from the street. But like the best of us, when the boss is away....At least you'll know she's there in the black house, and he's not. You only have those few days to make it work."

That month was the slowest ever. Truman went to Europe, met every official and his family, came back, toured South America, signed some laws, had a fishing vacation, tried to end that mess in Korea, couldn't manage to, played some piano, and decided to give it all up and go back to Missouri. It was that long.

Finally, the night came. I went there just after sunset. Doyle's street talk was on the money. The Towers had closed in on itself. The bungalow on the far corner of the estate was dark, empty. Marnie was in the mansion.

Climbing the big tree was easy. I'd done that sort of thing dozens of times. Watching nothing happen was the hard part. Hour by hour I felt the moss go damp around me. From midnight to three I watched eighteen goons patrol the grounds on horseback and in Jeeps. Then it happened, what Doyle had told me. Three guards went off duty for a half hour, leaving only six watching the back of the house.

It was the work of five minutes to jump down from

the tree on the inside of the wall, dash across the grounds, and start up an arbor next to the house. Before I got to the top, the popping sound I knew so well broke on my ears. The blue sedan, looking more like a jalopy than ever, screeched up the long drive and twirled in the gravel like a pretzel. Something was going on, and it wasn't good. Not good for Marnie. I needed to find her. I needed to do it now.

I reached an upper-story window high under the main tower, crawled under a ragged black awning, and slipped inside. The room was empty. I listened at the hall door. No sound there, either. Then someone squeezed it open from the hall. I dived into the shadows, and there he was.

A man — I thought he was a man. The eyes, sunk deep in their holes, were red and glazed; the brows were gone. He was new to me. One of the Order's new recruits? He had the broadest shoulders I'd ever seen. They filled the door opening. His arms were as thick as palm trunks, but his waist was impossibly teeny, like a debutante's on prom night. He wore a suit of blue tights and red boots. Fetching.

Slowly catching the silver light before him was a blade with a slight curve to it. A Turkish throwing dagger. Oobarab's toy of choice.

Ha! Here I was, noticing his get-up, and there he was, planning to kill me.

Was he talking? No. It was the chirping of Skull's annoying bird perched on the doorframe, its giant eyes staring into the shadows, as if to help Small Waist see into them.

Should I bolt? Could I get past him? Should I take him on just as we were? These thoughts flashed through my head one after another. Good thing my brain was having trouble turning over. In those few seconds I noticed that the Turkish blade wasn't his only weapon.

In his left hand was a gun so much larger than any gun I'd ever seen, it looked like a cannon. When I considered the size hole it would put in me, I started to ooze sweat like the fat man.

"Hey, boy?" the man whispered, as if calling a cat. "Hey...you gonna die now?"

I hated to be rude, but sometimes a question stumps you, and you just don't answer. I didn't move, didn't make a sound.

He did, though. Scanning the shadows, he said, "You there? Eh? Falcon? You ready ta breashe your lassht? Falcon? You ready ta die? Call it quitsh? Go kaputshki?"

"Not so much," I blurted out from the darkness of the room.

"Shut your lip!" he snarled. He fired at the sound of my voice. *Blam!* The window exploded behind me. I was on the move, though, and dodged the bullet, skidding flat and silent on the carpet behind a brocaded loveseat.

"Didn't get you, did I? Well. Shoon. Shoon."

He had kind of a boring style of threatening that I would have taught him how to do properly, except for that gun. It was a deadly piece of machinery I didn't want to be on the wrong end of. He could squeeze off a few rounds before I made it halfway out of the room.

And then what? Never see her again, never see her, never see my love ever again in this world?

There was a creak in the hall, and he twirled in his red boots. "Ahh ..." I heard him mumble to the hallway. "Shorry, Missh."

"What is it?" said a soft voice.

I nearly leaped out of the shadows. My heart did and went straight for her. *Marnie!*

"Intruder, Missh," he grunted. "But I'm taking care of 'im. You go back to your wing now, Missh. Ain't shafe for you here in thish part of the houshe."

The creak came nearer. "An intruder?"

Marnie's voice! There was pain in it, but something else, too. She knew it was me in there. She knew. It was all I could do not to jump out of the darkness right

then and pull her out of that chair and hold her to me!
Eight years since I saw you, Marnie! *My Marnie!*

Only before I could move, she spoke again.

"Fine. Send me a postcard when it's safe to come out."

"Eh? Missh?"

"They're taking me now to see some elephants," she said.

"Eh?" Tiny Waist repeated.

"Nothing, Stimp." She creaked away down the hall.

"Mad ash a bat," the man muttered to himself.

So Doyle was right. That horrible chair. The creak of the wheels. My heart beat for her. She was dying in Fang's clutches. She couldn't breathe in his strangle-hold. I had to get her out of there. But judging from the sound of four, five sets of footsteps thumping down the halls now, and the air-gulping roar of Malkin the tiger, that wasn't the time or place.

Before they crowded into the room, I dived through the open window frame, ripping the awning and break-ing several tiles — *crash!* I rolled across a lower roof and dropped into the bushes. Before I knew it, the tiger had leaped out the window after me, and a small army was chasing me across the lawn, firing madly.

I ran just as madly, climbing over the stone wall

like a lizard, and tearing down the sidewalk beneath the moss-draped trees. I gasped in huge breaths and almost choked. I could hear the sound of cloaks swishing in the night, and the musical *thoop* of daggers being drawn out of their leather sheaths and thrown. I nearly took one in the arm, but it struck a tree behind my head. Stimp lurched out of the shadows now, too. He growled a word — "There!" — and that cannon of his went off again. The thunder of the shot woke the dead only as far as Tampa. Before the smoke cleared, I dashed behind an early-morning milk truck, clung tight, and escaped.

When I heard the popping engine and screeching tires I knew why all the fuss. The blue sedan was racing away from the house. The Secret Order of Oobarab had taken her away, just like she said. "To see some elephants." *Oh, Marnie! My Marnie!*

"It might be days, weeks, years," I said to the lonely night. "But I won't ever stop."

With one last look at the castle, the growling of that sedan fading in my ears, I tried to imagine her angelic face, her eyes, but all I saw were Fang's bloated cheeks. When I tried to imagine her voice, all I heard was the *creak-creak-creak* of her rolling chair.

"You can't do this to her!" I shouted to the dark.

And that was it, right then. No longer for me, but for Marnie herself, I needed to find her. Life was empty until then. I needed to find her. Free her. Save her. Love her.

Nothing else mattered.

—*May 1952*

Gandy Bridge, Six Miles Long, Between Tampa and St. Petersburg, Florida

P-106

CHAPTER THIRTY-FOUR

Dia and I were stunned and silent. It was a long time before either of us spoke.

"This is not the end of the story," I said. "No way is it the end. We have to know what comes next. I have to know what happens. What do we do now?"

She was quiet, leafing through the pages, stacking them on her desk, leafing through them again. "I don't know. I don't know. I gotta think about it. Maybe by tomorrow I'll have an idea."

I read one line over and over.

No longer for me, but for Marnie herself, I needed
to find her.

And it happened to me, too. Sure, I needed to know
what happened to Nick and Marnie. Why was Fang hiding her? What accident crippled her? Why was he keeping
Nick away so fiercely? Did Nick find her? Did he save her?
But more than that, Dad needed to know. He needed to
know about his mother, and maybe his father, and I had to
follow the story to the end in order to tell him. Dia was
right. I think she was right. It didn't matter whether Emerson Beale was making things up. That's what stories
were. Things made up. It was still true. It was true, and I
believed it.

When I finally refocused my eyes, I found myself gazing at the rolled-up clothes scattered on Dia's floor.

She followed my gaze. "Jeez, you perv, get out of here!"

I didn't know what to say, so I left without saying anything except a laughing sort of, "Tell your mom great
meat loaf. Bye to your dad. I love those mal . . . mal . . ."

"Malangas. It's a tuber. Get out!"

I trotted to my house, thinking how strange Dia was.
She was always snapping at me — and the names! What

was *with* that? But I didn't care. It was the way she was. Dia was Dia. She was, I don't even know what.

My cell phone rang jarringly on the quiet street.

"Dude, you are not going to believe this," Hector said when I answered. He waited for me to say something.

"Believe what?" I said. "What is it?"

He made an excited noise with his mouth. "That word you told me about."

"Oobarab. What did you find out?"

"I Googled it, and guess what it means?"

My heart skipped. "What?"

"Nothing," he said. "Nothing at all."

I stood quietly on the sidewalk. It felt as if the whole story began to crumble in front of me. I felt betrayed. "Nothing?" I asked.

"Nothing."

It all seemed to tip the other way now. "Fine. He's changing things, anyway," I said. "A little kitten became this big growly tiger. A nice white house turned into a dark black castle. He's making it up. It's not true. So, okay. Oobarab doesn't exist. It's just a word, just a story. I guess I never expected it to be real. Dia and I hit a dead end, anyway —"

"Except," he said, then paused again.

"Except?"

"Well, try it," he said. "Try searching Oobarab on the Net. Dude, you'll laugh, you'll cry, you'll hurl!"

"I don't have a connection at my house. Tell me, okay?"

He made another noise, as if he could barely wait to tell me. "So, I key in the word, right? Man, I wish you could see this. And out of the whole Web, only a half dozen results come up."

"I thought you said the word doesn't mean anything."

"It doesn't mean anything. But you know what the top two results were?"

"Hector, I don't know what the top two results were!"

"Backwards," he said. "The results appeared backwards on my screen."

I didn't get it. "Backwards?"

"Backwards!"

I had never seen backwards results on a search. I couldn't imagine what they would look like. "What does that mean?"

"It means, my sunstroked friend, that the *word* Oobarab is backwards. Oobarab means nothing. But turn it around and it spells *Baraboo.*"

He waited.

I listened. *"And?"*

"And . . . Baraboo means something pretty incredible . . . especially for you down there . . . *right down there in Florida, dude!"*

"Like what?"

"Guess what it is. You never will. It's so mind-blowing, so incomprehens —"

"Hector!" I said. "Will you just —"

Suddenly, my blood turned to ice. The two lights I had left on in my house were out, and the narrow beam of a flashlight was jerking around inside.

"Holy crow!"

"Dude? What's going on?"

A shape moved past the windows in the Florida room.

"Hector, I'll call you later," I said, hanging up. I was terrified. I crept over to Mrs. K's house. Her lights were on. I tapped on the door. No answer. I knocked harder. Still no answer.

"Thanks a lot. *Now* you decide to go out —"

When I heard my back door squeak, I ducked into her flower bed, wishing roses didn't have thorns. Someone was outside now, and I could hear him moving away across my backyard. The bushes rustled. There was a distant squeak of a fence gate, a dog barking, then I heard a car start up and drive away from the next street over.

"What the heck?" I whispered. "A burglar?"

I couldn't believe it. I might have been in the middle of a mystery, sure, but not *that* kind of mystery. A burglar? That was too real.

I didn't move for a long time. I breathed huge gulps of air, but nothing else happened.

I knew if I called the police right away, my whole sketchy situation would be blown. Dad wasn't there, Mrs. K wasn't there. The police would take me to the station. They'd call Mom.

So what could I do? Even as I approached the house slowly from the side, I remembered all the times Hector and I had yelled at movie characters who investigate things they should have run the heck away from. I went still closer. I listened at the back door for another five minutes before doing anything. The door lock looked the same as the last time I saw it, but how could I tell if it had been picked? My cell phone was in my hand, already dialed to

9-1. Hearing nothing from inside, I twisted the knob and pushed in.

The door was locked.

Okay, this guy was either a good lock picker or he was just being polite, protecting my house against other burglars. I slipped my key into the lock and turned it. I pushed the door in a crack. Warm air came out at me. I stepped in. The house was dead quiet. I expected to see the place all torn up, but it wasn't. It was messy, but I couldn't tell if someone had been looking for something, if it were exactly the same as I left it, or — *weirdly* — if it were even neater than before. The boxes seemed stacked in a way that I didn't remember. No. Maybe not. I didn't know.

I checked Dad's room first. His wristwatch lay untouched on his nightstand. I walked through every room, even popping my head into the attic crawlspace. All empty. When I turned back toward the kitchen, I heard a crackle of noise that made me jump.

"Emergency, can I help you?" said a woman's voice.

"What?" I said to the dark.

"Hello?" the voice said.

I looked down. My fingers were clutched so tensely around my cell phone, I must have pressed the send button by mistake.

I put it to my face. "Hello."

"Emergency. Can I help you?"

"Oh, yeah, sorry," I replied. "I'm really sorry. I pressed 9-1-1 by accident. My phone is really sensitive."

"Can I have your name and address please?" she said.

I got nervous and hung up. *Was this going to be a problem? Could they track me down?*

I stood in the kitchen not moving for another few minutes, then walked three steps into the living room. Still shaking, I sat on the edge of the couch. "Okay . . . calm down . . ."

Hector had put a bug in my head and it kept flying and bouncing around. I called him back, but my call went to voice mail. Then I called Dia's house, hoping she might still be awake. The machine picked up.

"Dia, hi. It's me. . . ." I was going to add a name but couldn't remember her latest one for me. "When you get a chance, search the word *Baraboo* on the Internet. Hector thinks it means something important." I spelled it for her, then hung up.

I went over and knocked on Mrs. K's front door again. There was still no answer, but her lights were out now so she might have come home and gone to sleep. That's when I noticed a note tucked into the screen door. It read: "Jason, my key is where I told you. Lock the door behind you when you come in."

Where you told me? Wait, what did you tell me? The mailbox!

But her mailbox was empty. Why was it empty? Did she just write the note then forget to do what it said? I thought of pounding on the door, then of tapping on her window, but she would probably have called the police, if she even heard it, but I knew she took her hearing aids out at night. So I decided to go back home and just stay there. I'd already been burgled. What more could happen?

After two hours of walking around and doing nothing but listen to the faucet drip, I sank down on the couch, tired to my bones, and fell asleep. I woke up to the sound of the doorbell. It was morning. There was a policeman at the door, one I didn't know.

Emergency had tracked me!

"You're the boy with his father in the hospital, right?" asked the officer, consulting a small pad. His car idled on the street.

"Right," I answered, shaking. "I was just going to see him."

"Family Services said you weren't home yesterday when they came?" he asked, glancing past me into the room. "Everything okay here?" He leaned into the room now, then looked at his pad. "You're supposed to be staying with a Mrs. Kee . . . something; can't read my own writing. . . ."

"My neighbor," I said. "I've been next door since my dad fell."

"You know, I don't like this. It looks like you just woke up. Are you alone here?"

I shook my head. "No. I mean yes, but I came back here after breakfast, next door," I said. My mind began to race. He started to push his way past me, so I opened the door wide. While he was looking around, I hit redial on my cell phone, waited for a chirp of an answer, then hung up.

"We're packing things up," I said. "And cleaning stuff. To sell it. That's why it's messy. To sell the house."

"Uh-huh. And what about your mother?" He pulled his radio from his belt. "Is she down here yet?"

Okay. So what was Dia doing? Where was she? My cell rang. It was her.

"Hey, Roy," she blurted out when I answered, "did you just call me?" Not waiting for an answer, she went on, "Whatever. Listen. I searched *Baraboo* — that was you, right? On the phone last night? Anyway, you know what I found?"

The policeman was looking right at me. I drew a blank and only managed to silently put my finger up, to show him I was listening.

"Fine, Jerome," she said. "Baraboo is the name of a town in Wisconsin. If you're thinking so what, try this. Barabaoo is where the Ringling circus started. Ringling, Kiddo! Knife throwers. Skeleton men. Giants? Trained tigers? Alligators? Parrots!"

I practically had a heart attack. I still said nothing.

"Did you have a heart attack, or are you listening?" she said. "Plus — here's the second to biggest part — the huge Ringling house — a real giant castle — is in Sarasota about an hour from here! And you know what else? — here's the *biggest* biggest part — your great-grandpa Fang was chums with the Ringling family. Ta-da!" She paused a second. "Joey? You there? Ronny? Bob?"

I gulped. "Uh . . . hi, Mom."

"You freak!" she snapped from the other end of the phone. I imagined her in her room, sitting on the edge of her rumpled bed, her face smirking in the glow of the computer screen.

"Your mother's on the phone?" said the policeman, moving his hand as if to reach for it. "Can I . . . ?"

Dia whispered into my ear. "Hold on. Is someone there? I hear someone. Oh, my gosh! Is it . . . Fang? Mommy!" she yelled, "Fang's at Billy's house! Billy, blink twice if it's him —"

"Not yet, Mom," I said casually. "But the police officer wants to talk to you."

"What? Are you insane?" said Dia. "I can't talk to any —"

"Sure, Mom. Here he is."

I handed the officer the phone and hoped for the best.

"Hello," he said. "Mrs. Huff? This is Officer Perry. . . ."

I didn't hear what Dia said on the other end, but his expression didn't change. "I wanted to ask you — you are?" He began to nod. "Uh-huh, uh-huh. All right, ma'am, that sounds good. Please call us when you get here so we can . . . right."

He handed me the cell, and it was over. He looked around at the rooms once more and wrote a few more notes on his pad. "So she'll be here in the morning."

"Right. My mom," I said. "I can't wait. I miss her."

He leaned into both bedrooms. "So you haven't been staying here alone, then?"

"I, uh, no . . ." That was when the doorbell rang. It was Dia. She was completely out of breath. This time she was being Dia.

"Hi," she said brightly. "Everything okay? Did you sleep all right next door? Because if you didn't, my mom and dad said you could use our guest room tonight, and here's some stuff, if you need it." She held out a disposable razor (*what?*) and a pink toothbrush, probably hers. "I didn't know whether Mrs. K was tired of you or if you wanted to stay. Your mother's coming down soon, right?"

I was amazed at how good she was. Her bright face was so innocent and believable.

"Yeah, in the morning," I said. "Just after breakfast —"

"All right," said the officer, heading for the door. "Believe it or not, we have crimes going on in this city right now. Son, expect another visit from Family Services. And please have your mother call me when she gets here."

257

I said I would, and he left his number and extension and was gone.

"Man, you are awesome!" I said, stepping toward her, thinking twice, then stopping.

She pocketed the toothbrush and the razor. "You sounded in a bind. Plus, you look as pale as a pillowcase. A white one."

"I almost forgot to tell you!" I said. "My house was broken into last night."

"Holy —," she said.

"It really spooked me out, but I'm not sure anything was taken."

She glanced around. "How could you tell? Oh! Guess what else I found out? This is the best, best, best part. There was an article on the Ringling Web site written by guess who?" She stopped and smiled crazily at me.

"I don't know."

"Take a guess," she said.

"I hate guessing."

"Just guess," she said.

"Fang."

"Uh, no."

"The red-bearded German guy?"

"Vis a translation? No."

"Mr. Chalmers."

"Ha!"

"Look, I don't know —"

"Randy Halbert!"

S-58—Oranges Growing at Midway Groves, between Bradenton and Sarasota.

CHAPTER THIRTY-FIVE

I felt weak. "You're not serious. Randy Halbert? The real estate guy?"

"In which he mentions guess who? Quincy Monroe, that's who. They were friends, Monroe and the circus family. Well, not with Ringling so much, because he died in 1936, but the nephews and other people. Fang even stayed at their mansion when he wanted to get out of circulation for a while. Or, what I think, to hide Grandma Marnie!"

"Are you kidding me?"

"That's what I said! The Oobarabs in the story are circus people, totally. Plus they are totally real and have been following us. Well, you. And why are they following us? Well, you? I'll tell you. Because we're getting close!"

"Yeah, but close to what?"

She nodded, grinning. "Exactly! Something very big. I'll show you all the notes I took. I even downloaded a map of the Ringling estate. It took me forever. But not now; this afternoon. I have three lawns to mow before lunch. Maybe I'll even get to finish yours. Your dad's coming home soon, right? Why don't you visit him ever?"

"Visit him! I've been busy!"

"He's probably worried to death about you. You could at least call the poor guy, all busted up in there. Anyway, I'll be back in two hours. Sooner, if I don't have to rake." She flew out of there like a bird, chirping all the way down the street to her house.

I was more confused than ever. Not about calling Dad — I knew I had to do that — but about everything else. For the next ten minutes I tried to sort it out, but things were happening too fast to put them in order. It was muddled. Oobarab. Baraboo. Circus. Real estate agents. Yellow socks. Daggers! Tigers! Ringling! Burglars! *Dad!*

The kitchen phone rang. My ear was tired, and I was sick of this, but I thought it was Dia again so I answered.

"Dia?" said the voice. "Who's Dia? Why is your cell phone forever going to voice mail? Jason, what's going on down there?"

I sank to the floor. "Mom! Hi. Nothing. We're cleaning up. Dad's not here right now."

"You're *not* cleaning up," she snapped. "And the hospital called me. Jason! A concussion? His leg broken? This is very serious. Why didn't you tell me what was going on —"

"I'm fine. Dad's fine."

"He's not fine! I've been crazy trying to reach you. I told the hospital if I wasn't in London —"

"You're in *London*? When did you get there?"

"I'm taking the first jet back."

At that moment, I glanced over at the desk and saw the postcard that started it all, just sitting there flat. Man, all this mess from a little postcard —

I froze.

Wait. That's not right. No, no. I grabbed for my backpack and pulled out two cards, one of Sunken Gardens, the other of the Hotel DeSoto. *What? What!*

What was sitting on the desk? A new one? A *third* postcard? My heart began to batter my ribs again. I wanted to get to the card, but the phone cord wasn't long enough. Holy, holy. "Holy —"

"What did you say?" asked my mother. "Jason?"

"Nothing, Mom. Sorry, my cell is ringing across the room. It's probably the hospital. I think they want me to come. Dad's supposed to get out today. I'm supposed to go there to meet him. At two . . . forty."

"What?"

"I have to arrange for the taxi and stuff."

"Don't they have people to do that for you?"

"They do. That's right. That's what they said. We're pretty good right now. I've been staying with Mrs. K next door."

"Who? Mrs. Kay?"

"A friend of Grandma's," I said. "And also I've been eating dinner with a really a nice family. I've been cleaning the place up, and the real estate agent is probably bringing people in the morning, the first people to look at it. You don't have to come down here. I mean, you could, sure, but you don't have to right away —"

"Oh, I'm coming," she said. "The meetings aren't over until tomorrow late. In the meantime, your sister's on her way. This is so incredible. Jason, I can't believe you didn't call."

"Becca's coming?" I said. "When?"

"Tomorrow. Monday, I mean. It's Ray-Ray's birthday tomorrow." She sighed. "How much did he drink?"

"It was mostly an accident, Mom. He just fell. It was a lousy ladder. You know, Grandma wasn't into the best tools and stuff."

"Don't give me that. The doctor told me it was probably three or four beers. Thank God he wasn't driving you. Your poor father. I have to come. I just have to."

There was a silence next that dragged on a bit.

"Mom?"

"I'm here," she said.

"Mom. I'll have Dad call you. I'm going to talk to him soon."

More quiet on the line, then, "Call earlier rather than later. We're six hours later. Five. Whatever. Call me. I'll come as soon as I can. Expect Becca on Monday."

There were a few more words, but I couldn't tell you what. As soon as I was off the phone, I jumped across the room and snatched up the postcard.

Last night's intruder had left it. Of course, he did. Was

it another clue? Who the heck would break into my house and leave this? A friend? An enemy? An . . . Oobarab?

The card showed what looked like an enormous European castle, floating like an island in bright blue water. The castle had red tile roofs, dozens of arched windows, balconies everywhere, and fancy designs in the stones. I flipped the card over, hoping what it would say, but still stunned to read the words.

John Ringling Mansion
Sarasota, Florida

My knees turned to jelly. There was no address or postmark. All that was there, in clear marks made by a ballpoint pen, was this:

IV

Okay. Okay. Turning back to the picture, I lifted the card to the light, slowly, slowly. And there it was, a tiny twinkle of light near the top of the castle's tower, just under the tiled roof.

This was it.

I shook and shook and finally managed to call Dia again.

"Look, Barton," she said when her mother called her to the phone, "do you think I just pine around hoping you'll call? I was putting gas in the mower. For crying out loud, what is it?"

"I told you someone broke in here last night. I thought nothing was taken. And nothing was. But they left something behind."

She got quiet on the other end. "Not a . . . postcard?"

"Sarasota," I said. "The Ringling Mansion."

There was a scuffling sound like hands over the receiver for a few seconds. When she spoke again, she said, "I'm on my way."

CHAPTER THIRTY-SIX

The Ringling mansion was called *Ca d'Zan*. Dia said her father pronounced it: kah-dah-*zahn*. We suspected that going to Sarasota might be a trap — we were being lured there, after all — but there was nothing we could do about it. We had to follow the trail. Even so, we could use all the information we could possibly get. And Dia knew just where to go.

"Randy Halbert's office," she said.

"You know," I told her on the bus there, "you get everybody else's name right. Why not mine?"

She turned to me with a puzzled look on her face. "Wait, you have a name?"

"I wonder."

She smirked. "I wonder if you wonder."

I couldn't even tell you what that meant.

It was Sunday, but his office was open. As usual, when we pulled on the door, the air conditioning practically blew us back out onto the street again. His secretary sat alone at her computer, looking sour and sipping a foamy iced coffee from a domed plastic container. She said: "I'm sorry, it's Mr. Halbert's day off." Then she laughed a weird little laugh and said that real estate agents didn't have days off, so she wrote down where he lived. "Take a number fourteen and get off in Gulfport," she said. "He's a couple of blocks before Stetson U. Remember to say hi for me." She sipped her iced coffee, then added, "Nah, don't remember."

We took the bus, walked to 52nd Street, and found Randy Halbert's house. It was a small light blue box, well-trimmed and neat, with a new tile roof. We went up to the front door and rang the bell. A low-tide breeze wafted over us. The door creaked open.

"Is Randy —," Dia said.

"Shhh!" said a voice near her knees. A man on all fours was bent over the floor behind the door.

"Excuse me, do you need help getting up?" I asked.

"Hold on!" he grumbled, nudging the door closed with his shoulder.

We heard all kinds of shoving and scraping sounds. Finally the door swung wide. We faced a little old bald man with a dustrag rubber-banded over his nose and mouth like a bandanna. He looked like a bank robber, except for the reading glasses that gave him giant fish eyes.

"You want Randy," he whispered behind the cloth. "He's in there. And shhh." He gave a nod to the right.

"Thanks —," I started.

"I said, *shhh!*"

Giving each other a look, Dia and I stepped onto a large sheet of cardboard placed over the floor, which looked as if it were being retiled. We tiptoed into the Florida room. Randy Halbert was sitting on his couch amid a bunch of magazines, flipping through one of them. He looked up, but not quite at us, when we walked in.

"Jeez, kids. This is my day off. What are you doing here?"

Dia and I hadn't really discussed about how much to

tell him, but I felt we were getting close to something, so I told him pretty much everything — my grandmother, her boyfriend Emerson, the postcards, the Awnings, the Towers, the whole wild story. Finally I said that we knew about his interest in the Ringling house.

"Ten minutes," he said in a sulky sort of way to our waists. Then he waved his hand toward a pair of chairs, and we sat across from him. "I have to say, I'm kind of impressed," he said. "Not everyone makes connections between all the things you're talking about. So which one of you is the detective?"

"I am," we chimed together.

"Try to keep it down," he said in a hush. "Whisper, please."

Dia tensed up and scanned the rooms beyond us. "Why whisper? Is someone here? Is it Fang? Blink twice if it is!"

He didn't even blink once. "I'm babysitting my granddaughter. She's napping."

I got right to the point. "I need to know anything you can tell me about Quincy Monroe and my grandmother and any connection to the big Ringling house."

The agent glanced over at the old man, who was on his knees again scraping and tapping on the floor. When we heard the baby cry from another room, the man got up, and Randy frowned as if he were annoyed, then resigned to telling us what he knew. I think he wanted us to leave as soon as possible.

"The Monroe family," he said, "was one of the first great families of Florida's west coast. Boosters, they used to call people like the Monroes. The early land booms brought all kinds of people here. The Gulf Coast Railway was founded by Patterson Monroe and taken over by his son Quincy when he died. They scooped up land wherever they could find it. The Monroe Dynasty, they called it. Soon they were not only railroad barons, but had gotten into hotels, citrus plantations, residential housing. You following?" he said to my T-shirt.

We both nodded.

"This is Florida," he went on. "Finally it's all about land and Quincy had plenty of it, downtown, up and down the coast, what have you. When the first land boom ended in 1926 and the stock market crashed three years later, and the Depression came, landowners were caught like everyone else. Monroe was one of the few buying. He made shady deals, under the table, things that might be thought of nowadays as swindles, even hoodwinked the state, so they say. Florida was wide open and wild back then. What others had to sell to survive, he siphoned off cheap. It made him a lot of enemies. A scandal blossomed in 1933, I think. I want to say big scandal, but nothing happened. It was investigated, then went away. I think Monroe pulled a blanket over the whole thing. No proof. It was the kind of power he had."

I wondered about that. Was that why Nick's father wanted the newspaper that day? To find out about what happened in the state capital? That was about land and money. Nick remembered that that was back when he was nine. Maybe that was in 1933.

"Go on," I said.

"Ringling died a few years later," he said.

"In 1936, I read," said Dia.

Randy nodded. "There was a distant relative, a hanger-on, who stayed friends with Monroe. When the mansion, *Ca d'Zan,* opened to the public in 1946, this nephew kept his hand in close. He had parties there. Even lived there for a time during the off-seasons. Monroe and his family were visitors."

The old man, still wearing the dust rag over his mouth,

leaned into the room. "Emma fell back asleep in my arms," he said. "She'll be in dreamland for a good hour."

Randy snickered. "Didn't Great-grandpa's mask scare her?"

"It takes a lot to scare that little girl," he said with a sound like chuckling. "I'm gonna trim the hedge."

"Wear your hat. It's sunny out there," said Randy.

"Never leave home without it," he chirped. A second later, we heard the front door click.

"What about Emerson Beale and my grandmother?" I asked.

Randy shifted on the couch. "I know he was her boyfriend, but her old man didn't like him. Why is anyone's guess. Tried to shoo him away. After the accident in that crazy, experimental autogyro thingy, which Monroe blamed himself for since he was driving it, his vast empire began to crumble. He sold off pieces of it to pay for doctors, unorthodox treatments, procedures, going to clinics all over the world so that his daughter might walk again. He tried it all, gave her anything and everything —"

"Except what she really wanted," said Dia. "Nick Falcon."

"Emerson Beale," I said.

Randy shrugged, his eyes flicking nearly to my face, then away. "She was married to a man named Walter Huff. But he died overseas, they say. They had a son — your father — but who knows how she took care of him. The old man wasn't crazy about that, either. I get the impression she really loved your father as best she could, but she was so ill, disabled after the accident, and Monroe kept sending him off to schools and things. I can't imagine what that must have been like, but he's probably told you that already."

Dad hadn't told anyone, of course, not the whole story. Mom knew about Walter Huff being only a name, and she suspected Fracker of something not quite right, but that was only part of it. There were Dad's years as a boy living day after day with a sick mother and a cold grandfather. That was part of what he kept inside. That was the reason he was the way he was. It was so odd, and sad, hearing this from a stranger.

The room went quiet for a while.

Dia showed Randy the postcard of the Ringling house, and he smiled. "These postcards. Sometimes you can see buildings, places that don't exist anymore except on one of these cards."

He chuckled to himself in his usual way. "The strange thing I've noticed is how if you look at these cards long enough, the real world begins to take on these colors. The grass, the cars, the buildings. It's like the artificial becomes real. As for the Ringling estate," he said, handing the card back, "it's still there, and it's still like that. It's an attraction now, but I've been on the grounds of the estate when everyone leaves, and it's something you'll never believe. The whole *now* falls away when you're at that house. Old Florida comes alive out of the air."

Something I wanted to say then but just couldn't bring myself to, Dia blurted out. "But you're helping to tear down old Florida. The hotel, for one thing. And your luxury mall? The DeSoto Galleria? Are you kidding?"

He breathed in. "Right. I know," he said slowly. "The truth is, we don't live in the past. We can't. But you can love parts of it. And you pick and choose. This house, the house my wife grew up in, my father-in-law's house to begin with, she loved it. If you can believe it, it was originally built in one of Monroe's developments for his railroad workers. Nineteen-twenty-eight. We're restoring it to the way it was. Spanish style. Sarah's dad's helping me, as you see. And the mall will use fixtures from the old hotel, the columns, the woodwork. Which I made sure of. You pick and choose. And do your best."

Randy Halbert was looking at us now. "The best of it, of old Florida," he said, nodding at the postcard in my hand, "is in a place like that. It's so . . . beautiful."

Dia stood. "We want to go there. We need to go there."

He nodded. "I'd even take you, but my wife's out and my granddaughter . . ."

"That's okay," I said. "Thanks for your help."

"Watch out for yourselves," he said.

"Which reminds me," said Dia when we got up. "What exactly is the Secret Order of Oobarab?"

He snickered. "It was a group of circus folk who claimed to be the descendants of the real first circus from Baraboo, Wisconsin," he said. "Most of them never made John Ringling's cut. But they hung around and were perfect for Monroe. To do his dark dealings. If any of its members are still alive, they must be quite ancient by now. The Order must have long since disbanded."

"Not so much," said Dia. "The Oobarabs are back. Jimbo and I have seen them."

Randy frowned at our knees. "Who's Jimbo?"

"Me," I said.

Air View of St. Petersburg, Florida "The Sunshine City"

CHAPTER THIRTY-SEVEN

We took a Greyhound from the bus station and were in Sarasota in under an hour and a half. It had been hot all morning, but was cooler now that the sun was on its long drop into the Gulf of Mexico. It was afternoon by the time we passed under the pink arch of the gatehouse and into the visitors' center. We got the cheapest tickets we could that included a tour of the house — we were big on house tours by now — and walked out into the sun.

Thick, gnarly trees grew in clumps on either side of the paved foot path. They looked like muscles punching up from the ground. Dia said they were banyan trees. What I thought were vines dangling from the upper branches were roots, driving straight into the ground. Signs said not to touch them or we'd damage the trees. Palms with flailing leaves, woodpeckers, butterflies, birds sweeping and bubbling and cooing and chirping were alive over our heads. Ringling had grown a jungle around himself.

"Randy wasn't kidding," Dia said when we first glimpsed angular pink walls through the trees. "Look at that house."

House? *Ca d'Zan* was a fantasy palace, an enormous stack of pink boxes decorated with fancy stonework and balconies and arched windows and cutouts. It was like a cross between an old church and a wedding cake.

We walked slowly around to the back of the house, where rose-tinged stone glowed orange in the sun. The great wide *piazza* (a word from the brochure) spread out like an airfield of zigzagging marble stones surrounded by a thick stone railing as high as your waist. The greenish-blue water of Sarasota Bay gulped and splashed against the sea wall beneath us. If we were a hundred feet out on the water, looking back, we'd see the same image as on the postcard.

"The mansion was built in 1924," Dia said. "Ringling's

wife, Mable, really liked Venice. This house is like ones you see there." Doves warbled in the nearby trees, or maybe from the eaves. There were plenty of those.

I had been holding off — why, I'm not sure — but I now set my eyes firmly on the tower. The red-tiled roof loomed over us from what seemed like a mile away. A short outdoor staircase swirled from some inside room and swept to the top. The tower itself was an awesome piece of building, a square, open crown with pillars rising and splitting into fancy stone cutouts. A band of sculptures ran around the walls just under the roof. The tower was so clean and high and bright in the sun. I saw a woman's brown-haired head leaning out of the top with a camera in her face. It didn't look right to have regular people up there, but it was where Dia and I needed to be.

"Do you think Fang brought Marnie here? Hid her inside this house?" she asked.

"You mean, Quincy brought Grandma?"

"Same thing."

I looked at her. "So we've pretty much given up the idea that this is just a story? I keep thinking about the kitten and the tiger. And the Awnings and the Towers. What about them?"

"Details," she said.

I guess I believed that, too, and really just wanted to hear someone else say it. I only hoped we'd find the answers we were looking for. I was growing certain that the story was almost over. It was heading for an ending, and it was heading there fast.

"We need to get into the tower," I said. "Let's get on the tour."

"Yeah," she said with a grin. "I want to hear how somebody could build an Italian palace in Florida. Inside, Teddy, inside."

As the group gathered, Dia went up to the guide, a silver-haired older man whose name tag read *Dick*.

"Is the tower on the start of the tour or the end?" she asked.

Dick frowned. "The tower is not on this tour at all," he said. "You only see it on the Private Places tour." He glanced at our wristbands, then checked his watch. "The last one is starting at four. Another half hour. You still have time to run up to the visitor's center and get a ticket for that one. It's a green bracelet today. You'd be the only ones on that tour."

I gulped. "How much is it?"

"Twenty dollars," he said.

"Each?" asked Dia, and he nodded.

We dug into our pockets and came up way short.

He smiled. "I'm sorry. Maybe next time?"

Okay, this was bad, but Dia gave me a look that said she was already thinking of something. "It's okay, sir. We'll be happy just to see the fabulous rooms."

She was really good at getting us in and out of tours, and we tried to stay to the rear of the group, but Dick was always careful to round everyone up before moving on.

"This guy knows his stuff," she whispered to me.

The walls of the giant rooms were draped with tapestries and classical paintings. The ceilings were painted with legendary figures and scenes. We walked slowly from room to room as the guide told us about the Ringling family — there were five brothers; they started in Baraboo, Wisconsin; the house was built by John Ringling for his wife Mable and finished in 1926, but she only lived until 1929; and so on. I wondered again what my great-grandfather had to do with it all. Could he really have stayed here? Did he actually hide Grandma here?

Moments before we left the final room on the second floor, Dia nudged me and proclaimed loudly that she had to go to the bathroom.

"Excuse me, sir. I'm sorry. Is there a —"

"Bottom of the stairs and left through the kitchen," Dick said.

She nodded, then turned to me. "Joshie, come with?"

I smiled to myself, but grumbled. "Oh, all right!" We turned away from the group as it continued to another room, and made for the stairs. The moment they were out of sight, we jagged off to the left.

"Up the stairs," she whispered. "Sneak!"

I nearly laughed. "You're just a little criminal, aren't you?"

"Developing skills, Babe." We tripped quickly up a narrow set of curving marble stairs to the third floor. No one was up there. I guessed were were getting into the "private places." Going around the stairs again we came to a dark space. Bright white sunlight outlined the shape of the door. Dia tried it. Of course, it was locked.

"Except I don't think so," she said. Digging into a pocket, she pulled out a ballpoint pen. From another, she drew her library card. "Now, shhh. And don't tell the Mirror Lake librarian you saw me do this."

Her fussing seemed to take hours. I thought of Dad again and winced when I realized how many miles away from the hospital I was. I'd never called him, knowing that this whole strange adventure would end the moment I did.

"This is taking way too long. I should be with my dad —"

She turned to me, aghast. "You haven't gone to see him yet? My gosh, it's been, like, a month!"

"What?" I said. "How could I —"

"You should go. I'd be there the whole time if it were my dad, bringing him stuff. Iced Tea. *Sports Illustrated.* What the heck kind of son are you?"

I glared at her. "How could I have gone? I've been rushing around with you —"

Click.

"Finally!" I hissed.

"Like you ever break into places for us," she said.

"I didn't mean —"

"You never mean. Come on!"

When she pulled the little door open, it was as if we had been underwater and were coming up for air. Sunshine flooded over us. Pushing the door lightly closed behind us, we scrambled up and around the short, tiled staircase to the outside. Gulf winds rolled warmly over us as we stepped into the square room of the tower.

SA-H1065

CHAPTER THIRTY-EIGHT

West over the Sarasota Bay, beyond a wandering strip of islands, sat the big black broadness of the Gulf of Mexico. The breeze, constant and warm, smelled of seawater.

"Can I look at the card?" she asked.

I gave it to her. "The breeze is strong. Don't let it blow away."

"Right. Because I would do that."

That didn't bother me. Nothing bothered me, really. For — what? — three minutes? — for three minutes in that tower, I felt peaceful. All that had happened since I'd set foot in Florida was getting into my head. The old people.

The painted postcards. The little boxy houses. The sun and the heat. The lime-green grass, its smell when being mowed. I thought of awnings breathing in the wind and moss dangling from oak limbs. Palm trees, of course, their clattering leaves, whirring insects, sitting quiet in that dark, dark bungalow with Dia. All of it was seeping into me. Or I was seeping into it. We were seeping into each other.

I thought about it and thought about it, and then I stopped thinking about it and just let it wash through me like water through air. I was standing very, very still next to her, quietly amazed at how things were becoming different. . . .

"Holy *crikes*!" she said.

And the spell was broken.

I turned to her. "What's wrong with you?"

Dia was staring up at the roof on the water side of the tower and jumping up and down. "The tile. That tile! Look. The lady. The lady!" She turned me around and forced my head up. "There!"

Running all the way around the tower under the eaves was a row of painted designs raised in relief. There were flowers and vines and little horned, bug-eyed devil heads and bigger tiles of orangey stone with zodiac figures on them. The one on the corner to our right was a crab. The one above us was a lion. And there, next to the lion, was the figure of a lady.

She had wings. She was flying.

"Oh, man. Oh, man." My body went electric.

"You have to go up there," she said softly. "You have to get to that tile. That's got to be where he hid it. The story has to be there. It has to be —"

"I understand," I said. "Say it a few more times."

"So give me your foot," she said.

I looked at her. "Excuse me?"

"Your foot, Wilmer. The pinhole points to the flying lady. Of course, it points to the flying lady! Which means I have to boost you up there."

"It's a hundred-foot drop if I fall, you know —"

"More like sixty, but at that height it hardly matters. Your foot. Please."

There was no use arguing. Dia stood by an arch facing out to the water with her fingers laced together. With a deep swallow, I grabbed her shoulders, put one foot into her hands, and jumped up. The stone cutout nearest the corner was small, but I got a good grip on it and hoisted myself up. I put my feet on her shoulders. They were strong.

"Oh, man," I said, as she held my shoes with her hands.

"No kidding," she said.

Slipping one arm through the cut-out, I pulled up, leaving only one foot on her. I reached for the next cut-out and set the other foot on a carved decoration where the column blossomed up into the arch.

My heart was stuttering like a machine gun; my blood was icy. I couldn't imagine how many laws I was breaking right then. Not to mention the danger of it. But I tried to push those thoughts away, took a breath to calm myself, took another when that didn't work, then shifted my weight and brought my right foot onto the same little pedestal as my left. I was astonished I didn't just collapse to the floor, but I jerked my left arm and left foot to the next cutout and pedestal and swung my body over, hugging the stone tightly.

I was more or less under the flying lady now. She was naked and flying toward my right (south, I figured, though why I spent my brain working that out, I can't tell you). The blue area behind her was a series of flowery half circles. Waves, I thought. She was flying over water.

"Anything?"

"The tile's set into the tower. Maybe I can move it."

"Try," she said. "But don't fall."

"Because I hadn't thought of that," I said.

"You hush."

All this time, I was wondering why no one happened to glance up, see me, and start screaming. Maybe I was being quick about it? Maybe all these things were happening in minutes? Less? The sun was starting to lower into the Gulf, and the west face of the tower was glowing a brighter, more intense orange. Now my shadow was moving over the flying lady. *Over Marnie.*

"I guess I shouldn't tickle you now?" she said.

"Ha-ha." With my right hand, I reached up and touched the frame of the tile. It was solid. Of course, it was solid. The thing had been there for I don't know how many years. Through wind and hurricanes. Even assuming Emerson's story was ever hidden behind it, what if the tile had ever come loose in a storm and the story had blown away to nowhere? Huh? What then?

I moved my fingers all around the frame of the tile, pushing in and up with my thumb. It slid a little from side to side. My heart heaved into my throat. I pressed my fingers up under the bottom of the tile and tried to lever it out. It came a tiny bit, but only at the bottom of the tile. The top stayed in, as if it were hinged. This was good. I didn't know what I would do if the tile fell out and smashed my face. Or the lady cracked on the floor. Or on Dia's head. I glanced down at her.

"Eyes up, Pervo. You on vacation up there?"

Pervo? What? Jeez, always with that! I heard the thudding of doors below us. One, then another, then another. But the first one sounded nearer than the second and third.

"They're closing the house," she said. "Keep going."

I drew in a final breath and pulled out on the tile until it was open a good inch at the bottom. It stopped there. Working my fingers behind it, I felt at first only dust and rough stone. I edged my fingers upward as flat as I could —

"Owww!"

"What?" she said. "What is it? A booby trap?"

"No . . . ," I said. "A paper cut."

"Oh my gosh. You've found it!"

"You hush."

Paper was tucked in behind the very top of the tile. Pinching it between my first and second fingers, my knuckles scraping the stone of the tower, I tugged. Several sheets folded into quarters came out in my hand. I pushed the tile snugly back into place.

My heart was still drumming wildly. I lowered the pages to Dia. She fell back, leaving me hanging by one hand.

"Oh my gosh!" she said, "I'm sorry!" She tucked the pages into her pocket and reached up to me with both hands. I gave her one foot, locked my palm tightly into hers, then jumped down next to her, breathless.

Dia whipped out the pages and unfolded them, five sheets altogether, yellow and old, clogged with type on both sides.

A lone golf cart moved away down the long drive.

"The last tour is gone," Dia said. "This is the safest place to be now. Lori won't find us."

"Lori?" I said.

"The security guard. With the khakis and long hair."

I gaped at her. "You remember a guard's name from two seconds and you can't remember mine?"

"Read, Scooter. Read."

We dropped to the floor of the tower, our breaths still heaving, and began to read.

S.83—Alligators in Tropical Florida
Sarasota Jungle Gardens   3C-H858

CHAPTER THIRTY-NINE

IV

THE FLYING LADY

By Emerson Beale

Fifteen years of running, fifteen years of staying a step ahead of the Secret Order of Oobarab, had made me tired and wary.

I knew who they were now. Circus folk, friends of Fang, underworld employees, loyal to his madness, his rage. His army of goons and thugs had been after me from the first time I'd ever set eyes on Marnie. They wouldn't quit.

They must have figured by this time that I wouldn't quit, either. Marnie had been whisked away to France. Switzerland. Brazil. Hidden for years in clinics, hovered over by surgeons, prodded by spine specialists, priests, shamans, every one of them spending Fang's money, not every one of them helping her to walk again.

For seven years, I tracked them from the Towers. For seven years hid in the shadows. For seven years resolved never to stop.

Now Marnie was back in Florida, in Fang's clutches as tightly as ever. With the Towers only a dark memory, they were holed up in that wedding cake of a castle now.

I had to find her. I had to take her away.

Tonight was the night.

I waited in the car park across the road from *Ca d'Zan*'s pink gatehouse, scanning for any signs of movement. Birds twittered their good-nights. A jittery bat flapped its wings overhead and vanished. Inside the castle, Fang had gathered close his army of sad clowns and asthmatic strongmen, foreign knife throwers, bearded women, and aging rope walkers. In seconds, I would be among them in the heart of the enemy camp.

Across the pavement I ran, through the bushes, and over the estate wall in a bound. I crouched, froze, and listened. No one had heard me. Good. Moving in the shadows, I closed in on the big house. The evil fortress.

A guard slithered silently over the path. I ducked behind a monstrous cluster of banyans. A signboard cautioned against touching their sinewy roots, or you'd hurt the trees. I could sooner believe those roots would whip up and strangle you before it ever got to that. The grounds were nothing short of a jungle, except that this jungle had a trimmed path and the path was dotted with little stone cherubs. One of them was slowly being strangled by those roots as he sang for help. I guess he got too friendly and they weren't having any. Wishing him luck, I moved on.

Iron glinted in the moonlight near the house. One, two, three flashes of silver followed it. Together, they floated along the inside of the piazza wall and, after a moment or two, disappeared. My anxiety didn't.

"Oobarab?" I whispered.

"Oobarab," I answered.

Pulling myself together, I set off toward the caretaker's house at a quick sprint, hiding flat against it before the guard returned.

I had heard the stories. Of course I had. She's crippled. She's dead. She's married to someone else. She's in China. Fine. I'd go to China. Only she wasn't in China. She was right there. Fang had her locked up tight, and I was going to free her. Free her, and take her away.

I dropped below the wall of the surrounding hedge.

When the guard returned, he was humming softly to himself. It was the same Cuban tune I'd heard on the radio at that breakfast joint so many years ago. Silently, I thanked the guy. He was like a walking dance band, doing the horn parts and drums and all, serenading Marnie and me with what was probably our song, only he didn't know it.

Yeah, yeah, never mind, Nick. Focus. Focus.

Ten minutes later, I was standing flat against the big house. Something silver flashed by my head, fell, and clattered to the stones. I dropped to my knees, not hurt, but startled. On the ground near my feet was a long knife — a Turkish throwing dagger. Instinctively, I jumped up and ran. The circus wannabes had the same idea. Gosh, there were a lot of them, and they were suddenly everywhere, as if they had sprung out of the ground, children of the Hydra's teeth. I tore back into the trees, but they knew that trick. A branch snapped, a heel twisted, I spun quickly and went down like a sack of lead.

When I came to, I was trussed up like a hog awaiting slaughter. Only this time, I wasn't in a boat. Two beefy giants in oily suits and a hefty silver chain held me down in a thick velvet chair on the wrong side of a big oak desk. The mantle behind it was wide and long enough to land a plane on. At one end sat that parrot, glaring at me before swiveling its tufted head to the doorway. The next thing I knew, Fang was there, fatter and sweatier than ever. When he turned his face to me, it was wrecked, inhuman. A seven-inch scar sliced down from his forehead, across his right eye, and onto his upper lip.

The accident did this to him?

He leaned over the desk at me, his dead eyehole as deep and dark as a coal mine at midnight.

"Maybe it's something...types like you have...," he said, huffing at me.

"Good looks?" I said.

"Something that just won't...give you a clue," he said, ignoring that. "Because if you *had* a clue...you'd know that if you talk to her...even see her...I will stop her treatment. I'll cut it off, just...like that. She'll never walk again, boy. Soon, she won't move at all —"

"That's insane!" I said. "She's your own daughter! Are you mad?"

His horrible eyeless, lifeless socket seemed to stare at me from its depths. He said nothing. But at that moment, I wouldn't have heard anything, anyway.

She came swimming past the window as if on wings. She touched down outside and watched the whole scene. Was she floating above the piazza stones? Was she flying?

Did she have wings, purple and rose and blue in the twilight?

No. The tears in my eyes were making everything blur. The squeal of her chair brought me out of that trance. Skull Face wheeled her past the room. Tubes all over her. The sound of oxygen spurting, doing her breathing for her.

"Marnie!" I said.

The chair receded. She was gone. *Had Marnie seen me? Heard me?* I didn't know.

"Don't dare speak her name!" Fang bellowed, his vast bulk wobbling. I wasn't prepared for what came next. He made as if to sit, then came at me, cupped my face with his left hand, and whipped me with his right, hurtling Marnie's picture from his desk to the floor, shattering it.

When my head whipped back, I saw bodies bouncing high over the piazza. A half dozen costumed acrobats rehearsed on a trampoline.

"You don't . . . you don't get it, do you, boy!" said Fang, pulling my face back to his, breathless after all that exertion. "I know all . . . about where you come from. You're not fit to be with her. You're a dirt kid, a dirt kid . . . and I'm . . . I'm Florida!" The parrot squawked that last word out as if someone had squeezed its toes in a garlic press.

"Florrrrrrdaa!"

I acted as if that meant nothing to me. As if it didn't hurt, coming from him. But it did hurt, even coming from him. *Not fit to be with her.*

"You can't stop the two of us," I said.

"Ha!" he snorted. "Her accident twelve...years ago stopped the two of you! Besides...she was never yours to begin with, and she certainly isn't now!"

"Fang, you soulless zombie!" I said bluntly, struggling against the cords on my wrists. "You walk, you talk, but you're a ghost inside, a cold-blooded serpent—"

From deep in his throat came a sound like the roar of a tiger in reverse, or a dragon's death rattle. *"Kaaah!"*

If I could have jumped, I would have. It was an ungodly cry. He heaved forward, thumping his great fat palms on the desktop. "Better," he screamed, "better—than—actually *being* dead—*kaaah!* Which is what you'll be! Dead! Dead! Dead! *Mr. Stimp!*" He flopped back into his chair like an avalanche coming to rest.

The tramping of steps came soon enough. Mr. Stimp, the muscle-bound, cannon-toting freak I had escaped at the Towers, came staggering in.

"Is he going to drive me home now?" I asked. "Or just throw me in the general direction?"

"Mr. Stimp," the fat man said, his huge stomach

wobbling inside his jacket, "please arrange for Mr. Falcon to do some ... traveling."

One gray tooth, chipped to a V, peeked out from the side of Stimp's mouth. "I'll pack him in hish own shuitcashe, ssssshir!"

"A suitcase shaped like a coffin!" said Fang.

They both burst into a good old laugh at that. It was a funny routine, but I didn't wait for the next joke. I had been fooling with the chain behind my back and now ripped myself from the chair, kicked out at the twin Beef Boys, and swung the chain hard at Mr. Stimp. He hollered and stumbled. Amid the parrot's squawking and Fang's shrieks, I dashed from the room.

The strongman swore and came after me, leading with his howitzer. In no time, the whole crew, the deadly Secret Order of circus freaks, was tramping down the mansion hallways after me.

I crashed out through a set of doors, rolling out onto the great piazza under the tower. Evening had fallen orange and blue across the colored stones. I raced down the steps toward the water, thinking to swim for it, when I heard a sudden cry.

"Nick!"

I turned, looked up, and there was Marnie. She was wearing a flowing gown of pastel green. Its skirts fluttered at her bare feet like tail feathers.

She was held up by Mr. Tall and the German like a limp ragdoll just inside the tower railing.

The whirring of blades in the air above us — *flack-flack-flack!* — was nothing less than Fang's terrible autogyro. Skullface was driving the thing.

Fang had wobbled out onto the piazza now.

"She's leaving you — forever!" he crowed.

"You're mad!" I cried out.

Cursing, I started toward the tower, when Fang shouted again. "Mad, am I? You'll never learn what happened over the Bay! Never! Kaaaah!"

I ignored that until I heard a splash. Then came the slap of wet feet on the stones behind me. I turned. An alligator was sloshing up the steps from the sea wall. No, make that a dozen alligators, each as large as a yacht. Their jaws grinned horribly in the moonlight. But it wasn't just a beauty contest. At Fang's call, they galloped across the stones toward me.

The rest of the Order stood watching, Fang laughing in their center like a demented king, his fat hand signaling the autogyro to descend, its rope ladder swinging wildly above the tower.

They all watched as, inch by slithering inch, the hungry gators approached.

"And now for The Big Show!" Fang bellowed. "Eat, Gators, eat!"

Seeing Marnie up there broke my heart. She was as frail and limp as a marionette, without a power of her own. They were taking her away forever.

My mind flashing back, I remembered words my old pal Harrow had told me once. He said if they worked at all, it was nothing short of a miracle, but I needed a miracle now. Whispering the words, I heard — even above the thrashing of the autogyro's blades — a distant crumple of tin and wood. And they came.

They came.

Fourteen elephants stampeded across the lawn to the big house. They bellowed and trumpeted at the top of their immense lungs. The night burst into a thousand pieces, then came together again with their great loud song.

The beasts thundered onto the piazza. Trampling across the stones, they sent the alligators diving toward the water.

Fang shrieked loudly to his goons in the tower. "Kaaakkk-ak-ak —"

I had to think fast. Heaving myself to the back of the lead elephant, I stood and jumped at the trampoline.

Yelling, "Marnie!" I dropped fast, then bounced high, hurling myself straight to the tower's steps. In no more than a half second, I bounded up, slipped my arms around Marnie, and pulled her away from the goons.

"Nicky!" she cried, her arms suddenly alive in mine.

"His hate poisoned you!" I said. "His lies. His madness. He kept you in that chair! But you don't need it anymore. I'm taking you away. Come with me now!"

The elephants were attacking the thugs now. You should have seen the circus freaks scatter! Where she got the magic, I don't know, or care, but Marnie leaped from the tower and floated us down hand in hand to the shadowed lawn, the wings of her gown fluttering like a sea breeze through the wild palms.

"That was close," she said, when we lighted on the ground.

"Not as close as I want to get with you," I said.

"Aw, shucks, you charmer!" she sang.

"I learned that elephant call from a witch doctor pal of mine," I said.

"Which doctor?" she said, and her laugh was like the sound of chimes across that flowery evening.

Whistling a call to the lead elephant, I grabbed its trunk and flung myself onto its back, leaned over, and pulled Marnie up to me. She was as light as a feather.

But it wasn't over yet.

Fang bellowed like a hurt cow. Shots rang out, chinking against the paved path, and a dozen matching daggers whizzed past our heads. Marnie pushed me low, and the blades clattered harmlessly to the grass as we thundered across it. We slid off the beast at the gatehouse and flew across the street to the car park.

I glanced at her face, her hair flying in the breeze, and knew it would never end.

This was it for me. I had freed my Marnie. She was mine. I was hers. Forever. Forever.

The park was empty except for two cars — Fang's empty chariot (cream-yellow, chromed, washed and waxed, top down) and the crumpled blue sedan I'd seen too many times before. We started for the convertible, then slowed.

"Wait," I said, sensing a change from behind us. No footsteps, no footsoles echoed on the walks. No thudding on the lawn. The street, quiet.

"But they're coming —"

"Not anymore," I breathed. "They're here."

For a moment, nothing happened. Then it came. Metal squealing horribly as two doors on the blue car flew open at the same time.

"I had to be right, didn't I?" I whispered.

Marnie held my arm. It was the touch of a love that had held strong for such a long time. The air was alive with love and danger. So were we.

When the closer man got out, the car bounced sudden and high on its shocks, relieved that it no longer had to bear his immense weight. It was a man I hadn't seen before. He was the size of a house.

"Golly, he's big," Marnie said flatly.

"Uh-huh," I said. "How fast can Daddy's car go?"

"In my mind, we're already around the corner," she said, flying for the cream-colored chariot.

Running right after her, I laughed. "I love that mind!"

And not only her mind.

The giant and his friend evaporated in the distance like a bad dream. We raced the car for hours and hours until morning broke over the Keys at a little place I'd always loved called Twin Palms. I can't remember now whether I carried her to the beach or she flew us there, but we didn't leave for hours.

"I think I'll stay in your arms forever," she said when we woke up on the sand.

I smiled at her. "Yeah, you will."

— *July 1959*

The story ended there. Two yellow papers were stapled to the last page. They were legal documents, dense and serious and too faint to read in the darkening tower. But there was no more story.

"That's it?" I said. "Where's the rest? What happened?"

I turned to Dia. She was smiling. "Unbelievable. So cool. Awesome."

"What?" I said. "Like all that could really happen? Trained alligators? Elephants? Magic words? He bounced up and grabbed her, and she flew them to the ground? *Flew* them? None of this could happen!"

She searched my face. "Maybe it couldn't happen, but it could still happen."

"What? No," I said, thinking she had read something I hadn't. "That's not the end. It can't be the end —"

I couldn't tell if her look then was one of annoyance or of pity. "Goofus," she said quietly, "it's what you've been thinking all along."

"I've been confused all along!"

"It's what you've been hoping for. *Who Nick is.*"

"What —?"

Loud popping and rumbling exploded in the air. Peering out of the tower, I think I squealed like a first grader. "Diaaaa —"

Together we watched something the size of a small

304

yacht careening over the tram route, smoking and hissing and growling.

Every inch of the car was dented, and the windshield had a whole alphabet of cracks across it. But I knew right away it was the same car we'd been reading about.

It was the blue sedan.

4A-H806

CHAPTER FORTY

"Wow, full circle," Dia murmured. "From the first story to the last."

Full circle. That's exactly what the car did. Three times. No sooner had it crashed up onto the piazza, than it spun around and around and around across the stones in a doughnut and came to a wobbling, bobbling, screeching, squealing halt.

"It's amazing that car still drives," she said. "Will you take a look at that thing —"

"Will you *run?*" I said. But by the time we leaped down onto the stairs, it was already too late. The little door leading inside was locked tight. Down below, the car doors swung open with a grinding shriek, and a glint of silver flashed in the fading light.

"A Turkish throwing dagger!" I gasped.

"Uh, actually," she said, squinting down, "I think . . . it's a leg."

The flash of silver touched the stones. I made another of those squeaky gasps. "Are you saying he has a silver wooden leg!"

There was another flash, followed by two more. There were four silver legs. It was a walker. Holding onto the walker was a man — I *think* it was a man — with a saggy bare chest and saggy blue tights and red boots. It was Mr. Stimp, the strongman! After him, a tall man — Mr. Tall, the giant! — unfolded himself from the backseat. The car heaved like a ship emptied of its cargo, bobbing on its tread-less tires. The tall man staggered to get his balance, then walked toward the water, his arms out, muttering, "Show me where! Point me at him! Beale, I'll stomp ya!"

The car still wasn't empty. The veiled purpley woman clambered out next, as low-cut as ever. The parrot flut-tered from behind her head and landed on the roof of the car. The round, red-and-gray bearded man rolled from the front seat like a barrel, tipped over, and was helped up by the man with the walker.

"Sank you!" the round man said, making an attempt to click his heels, but staggering again, this time against the sedan.

"Will you look at that," Dia whispered.

"I'm looking, I'm looking." I couldn't move.

Finally, there came a *thump-thump* — "owww!" — from behind the wheel. This was followed by an agonizing creak, and the driver's door burst outward and fell with a *clunk* to the stones.

The rest of the crew turned and watched as a black shoe toppled out onto the piazza. A foot in a droopy yellow sock emerged from the front seat, groped for the shoe like a blind man with his cane, found it, twisted into it, and clomped down on its heel. Following the shoe from the car was a very thin man in sunglasses with a face like somebody dead.

"Mr. Skull!" I said.

Mr. Skull raised his thin hand up over his eyes and squinted every which way. He saw nothing until the purple lady removed his sunglasses. Then he saw us in the tower. "Them we get. Now we get. Them!"

When no one moved, he added: "Oobarab!"

"What did he say?" said Mr. Tall.

"Oobarab," one cheered, then another did, then they all did.

Dia turned to me. "This is so very weird."

Together the Secret Order of Oobarab attacked us. At least, I think it was an attack. It was very slow. To be fair, we almost had to wait for them to catch up. They helped one another across the stones from the car to the house.

"That boy knows everything. Stop him!" said the veiled lady, her veil fluttering, her purple gloved hand waving toward us.

"Ve'll get you!" shouted the German dagger specialist. "For ze Order of ze Oobarab!"

"Oobarab!" some of them hooted again.

They weren't fast, the Secret Order, but they didn't stop, either. They jammed themselves into the house and, amid someone's calls for the elevator, started up toward the tower. As slow as they were, they had somehow trapped us up there. With sheer numbers, they could overwhelm us. My heart was thumping in my chest.

Dia leaned toward me in the dying light. "The rooftops."

"What about them?" I asked, already afraid of the answer.

"Run over them to escape?" she said.

"Are you crazy?" I asked.

She gave me a look. "Are they?"

"You have a point. Let's go. You first."

So we climbed over the railing in the very same spot that the goons had once held Marnie. The shortest — but not all that short — drop to the nearest roof was at least eight feet.

"Hey!" shouted the dagger man, bursting from the door first and onto the stairs toward us. "Zat's too danjeroo for kidz!"

"No, we're okay," said Dia. "Thanks, though!" Her palm held out to me, she grinned. "Thoughtful, isn't he?"

I grasped her hand firmly and together we slid across the roof tiles to the edge. We lowered ourselves to the next one down and from there to the balcony of a bedroom.

"They lived in separate bedrooms, you know," said Dia. "John and Mable. I read it in the guidebook."

I glanced at her. "Thanks for the tidbit." Hanging down carefully at first, then jumping wildly, we dropped onto the piazza and raced across it as the red sun — as red as the throat of that hummingbird in Grandma's backyard — disappeared finally into the bay. I think that despite every-thing, I may have laughed then. It was really too beautiful to do anything else.

The air was alive, and this was it.

I knew this was it. What *it* was, I couldn't say. But I was sure this was it.

We raced across the lawn toward the gatehouse when we heard the sedan popping and hissing again. Even though the chase seemed to happen in slow motion, it wasn't long before Skullhead cut us off and forced us past the cherub being attacked by banyan roots into an garage area behind the caretaker's house.

The yard was fenced in. There was no way out.

"This place we know good!" whooped the yellow-socked driver.

We were trapped by the Secret Order of Oobarab, a gang of the oldest and slowest, never-quite-actual circus people you could imagine.

"Geev it up, kinders!" said the knife thrower, hustling over to us. "Za papers! Now!"

They moved closer, pushing us flat against the fence.

"Um . . . no!" said Dia. She snatched the pages from me and stuffed them into her cutoffs.

The Oobarabs looked at one another. Without knowing exactly what to do, they staggered toward us menacingly. Mr. Stimp tugged his giant gun from a giant fanny pack on his tiny waist and rested it on his walker, aiming at us.

"Trapped!" said the purple lady with all the curves.

All of a sudden, something round and black and soft flew down from the roof of the caretaker's house. It caught the barrel of Stimp's gun and dangled on the tip of it.

It was a beret.

CHAPTER FORTY-ONE

The Oobarabs gasped, muttered, grumbled, and looked up.

"Ha . . . hal . . . halt!" coughed a voice.

It was the old beret-wearing man from the funeral home and Sunken Gardens, standing on the roof of the garden shed.

Seeing him there, I suddenly recognized him. He was the guy with the fish-eyed glasses and dust bandanna working at the real estate agent's house. "You're Randy Halbert's father-in-law!" I said. "The man with the tiles!"

"Wait . . . tiles?" Dia said. "Then you must have hidden

the story in the tower. And probably in the hotel bath-room, too! You're Doyle from the story —"

"Chester Howell Dobbs!" snarled Skull, as if they were old enemies.

"A name that strikes fear!" said the old man hoarsely.

The purple-veiled woman wobbled on her heels. "Oh, Dobbsy!" Then something else came to me. "Wait a second. You broke into my house and left this postcard for us to find. That's why we're all here!"

"Oh, no, dear," said a voice. "That was me."

Stepping up behind Chester Dobbs on the roof and clutching his arm was none other than . . . Mrs. K!

"Hello, Jason!" she said with a little wave of house keys. "Don't worry, dear. I turned lights on at your Grandma's house and locked it up snug as a bug."

I stared at them in shock. But there was more.

Everything around us seemed to rustle and snap then, and old folks staggered out of the bushes and from behind the pink house in ones and twos like the unburied dead. Standing together against the Oobarabs, they introduced themselves as war veterans and mystery writers — there was even a cook with an apron from the old breakfast diner! I recognized some of them from the funeral home.

They were Nick Falcon's — Emerson Beale's — old friends.

I slumped to the ground, not knowing whether to laugh or cry or scream. I whispered softly. "Holy cow."

I wished Dad could see this. All these people — Dia and I, too — were here at this moment because of Marnie and Nick, Grandma and Emerson, his mother and her boyfriend.

"What do you want the story for?" asked Dia, pulling the pages from her cutoffs.

"Not the story," said the purple lady. "The deed."

"The deed?" I said, taking the papers from Dia now. I scanned the last two pages but still found them impossible to read. "What does it say?"

"Dear, it's a deed to three miles of waterfront property," said Mrs. K.

"Worth millions!" said Skeleton. "And it's ours. To Oobarab it belongs. Quincy Monroe deeded us the land if his daughter Agnes died. It's ours by right of law. It's why we been after you!"

"Ve knew Beale must hev hidden zis deed," said the German. "Und ven Shtimp trailed you to ze hotel, ve knew

315

you ver on ze trail und vood lead us to it. Zo, ve came efter you."

I was shocked. "So it's all about . . . land?"

"Oh, Jason, dear," said Mrs. K, clearing her throat. "It's all right. Give the man his deed. It's nearly worthless now, anyway."

"Verseless?" cried the German.

"Kidding is what you've got to be!" said Skull, his jaw dropping open.

Dobbs tapped his pockets. "Dang. Where is it?" Then he rubbed his head. "Oh. Mr. Stimp. The beret."

The tiny-waisted man turned the beret upside down. Tucked inside it was a letter. He gave it to Mr. Tall who handed it up to Dobbs.

"It's from the old man's lawyers," said Dobbs. "The land *was* worth millions. Three miles of bayfront property in Tampa and St. Pete were owned by Patterson Monroe, Quincy's father. He leased it to Pinellas County a long time ago and, my friends, they built Gandy Bridge on it! The lease meant millions of dollars paid to its holder."

"Millions!" Skull repeated, his eyes twinkling icily.

Chester Dobbs shook his head. "Except that it was a hundred-year lease, signed ninety-six years ago. And the amount paid the owner of the land was less and less until, after a hundred years, the land reverts to the county, lock, stock, and barrel. The deed is worth only a few thousand dollars now," he said. "You can fish on the land for free, of course. But then, so can everyone else." It was quiet for a long time, except for the occasional sweep and flutter of bats over the darkening lawns. All of the Oobarabs looked at the yellow-socked man. Skeleton tensed for a minute, his mouth quivering. Then he slumped his shoulders, glumly kicking the grass with his old shoes. "Oh, what's the use? Worthless? We knew the terms of it. We may be circus folk, but dumb we ain't."

"You knew the deed was nearly up?" Dia said, astonished. "But if you knew, why did you chase us all over the place to get it?"

The Oobarabs glanced at one another. No one spoke.

Finally, Dobbs said, "Maybe I know why. The Order's been waiting for a chance to reunite. To take up the chase one last time. To live the old days again. The world doesn't have much use for people like us anymore. Until the deed was found, the story really wasn't over. It was a reason to start going again and to keep going. The same reason to keep going that I felt. That we all felt. Am I right?"

"Keep going," murmured Mr. Tall, gazing over at the cherub tangled in the tree roots. "It's a good reason."

"For ze danger und ze glory!" the German knife thrower added.

"So you'll take your thousands and stop chasing our friends here?" asked Mrs. K.

Skeleton shrugged. "Sure. No point now. Nice kids they look as if they are. But don't blab it. The Oobarabs are back together again. And they have iron hearts."

"Oobarab!" said Mr. Stimp, raising his arms high.

"Oobarab," said the others, not quite in unison.

"Thank you," I said to them, not sure that any of it made sense to me yet. "By the way, sir, what's your real name?"

"Scully," he said, shaking my hand.

There was no fight, no rumble of berets and spatulas and walkers. A calm settled over everyone, and we slowly made our way back to the piazza together. The sun had dipped below the dark Gulf. We sat along the railing by the bay, all of us, quiet under the bluing sky.

"Of course, we all knew about Quincy Monroe and the way he kept his beautiful daughter," said Mrs. K. "But Emerson was the only one to try to do something about it."

"You can't scare a man with a love like that," said Dobbs.

"Ve twied to," the knife thrower sighed, rubbing his shoulder and introducing himself with an almost click of his heels as Heinrich Punch. "Ach, I can't srow no more."

"You were da besht," said Mr. Stimp, biting off the barrel of his enormous pistol, which turned out to be chocolate. "You were."

"Sank you much," he said. "I never wealy twied to hurt himp. He must heff known zis, no? I vanted only to shcare himp."

"You didn't much," said Dobbs. "Never mind what he wrote in his story. You were always a menacing terror in the story."

"I like to sink zo," said Punch.

Scully shook his bony head. "Boy, oh, boy. You can't scare a man with a love like that, I always say!"

"*You* always say?" said Dobbs. "Everybody steals from me. . . ."

"But the story," I said. "Was any of it true?"

The bunch of them looked from one to another and back again.

"Beale wrote bizarre mysteries," said Dobbs finally.

"But maybe there was a lot of truth in them. Old Monroe was an angry and twisted man, sure he was; but maybe all he really wanted was for the daughter he loved more than anything to be well again. Love will drive some people to amazing things."

The purple lady sniffled under her veil, then sneezed, and a furry thing fell to the ground at my feet.

Dia picked it up. It was a fake beard.

"Well, there goes the act," said the woman, pulling her veil off to reveal the kind-looking face of an attractive older lady.

I recognized her instantly. "You were the lady at Sunken Gardens! You wore pink! And yellow!"

She shrugged. "Every now and again I need a break from Madame Olga, the Amazing Bearded Lady. Besides, you get tired of purple, purple, purple all the time. It's Marcia by the way. You know my son, Timmy."

"I do?"

"He's assistant director at Brent's," she said.

I gaped at her. "Mr. Chalmers?"

"Here," said a voice from the shadows. The pasty-faced man who had first said the name of Marnie walked out to join his mother. "Sorry about your grandma," he said to me.

I looked over at Dia. Her eyes were wide and glowing and moist in the fading light. Everyone was quiet for a while until Dobbs spoke.

"I guess there's nothing left to do now but take you to Bay Pines to see where he's resting."

"Bay Pines?" My heart sank. It was where Grandma was buried.

Dia put her hand on my arm. "Oh, Jason . . ."

I looked down at the pages in my hand. "You mean, after all this, we're going to the cemetery?"

CHAPTER FORTY-TWO

"I said where he's resting," said Dobbs. "Not where he's dead."

"Bay Pines Veterans' Hospital," said Mrs. K. "It's where Nick is —" She suddenly squinted around through her glasses. "Dang! Here comes security!"

"They run us off always," said Scully.

"Hey, you!" came a shout, then the sound of footsteps. "Are you geezers out there again? The estate is closed!" Then softer: "Unit Three, requesting backup. Unit Four —"

"It's Lori! Let's scram off!" said Marcia Chalmers.

"Scat!" yelled Dobbs.

"In my mind, I'm alweady awound ze corner!" said Punch.

We raced to the blue sedan and piled inside. It was actually very roomy. We tore away at top speed, laying rubber — as if there was any left to lay! — on the winding drive. We screeched around the visitors' center, then sliced over the grass and under the gatehouse arch, chased by a couple of whirring golf carts and the shouts of the estate security.

We hurtled through the streets of Sarasota, groaning and shrieking like a herd of elephants and parrots, then careened onto the highway north to St. Petersburg.

"He-he!" cried Heinrich. "Ze old bomp, she still gots it!"

When we were safely tooling along the highway, Scully turned to me. "About Marnie," he said, "that something fishy was going on, we knew. Before she got it, the old man wanted to see all her mail. Lots of postcards. Very fishy."

"Oh, that reminds me," said Mrs. K. She opened her purse, took out a stack of old colored postcards, and gave them to me. There must have been fifty or more of them. It was a collection of all the sights in St. Petersburg.

"Wow," said Dia. "What a stash! My dad would love to check these out."

"Nick sent your grandma many over the years," Mrs. K said to me. "I kept them all for her. But that one . . ." She tapped the card of the Hotel DeSoto still in my hand. "That was the first. She'd never part with it." The woman smiled sweetly at me, but with a faraway look in her eyes, as if she was remembering something from long ago.

By the time we screeched into the parking lot of Bay Pines Veterans Hospital, barely half an hour remained before visiting hours were over. A large new hospital was surrounded by a kind of wandering campus of older Spanish buildings and lush, green lawns with very tall pine trees and oaks and palms. Bay Pines was like heaven, a resort, even, except for the sick people. Older men and women, mostly men, from Vietnam and Afghanistan and the Gulf Wars, I guessed, were taking the night air in the park outside the main entrance. Many were in chairs, some had canes. Some younger men stayed to themselves, staring out with vacant looks, while others laughed in small groups.

Dobbs sighed. "Emerson can't leave here anymore. Malaria from Japan did in his lungs and ticker. Can't see outta one eye, and the other's no telescope, either. All that running and jumping over the years didn't help. Life finally caught up with him. He has me do his roundabout work for him."

"You still gots it, too!" said Heinrich Punch as we rolled into the wide circle in front of the entrance.

Dobbs tipped his beret to the little German. "Emerson's living under another name. Nicholas Falcon, if you can believe it. Don't ask me how he pulled that off or where he got the identification papers or the photo ID. I haven't the faintest."

"Oh, I can't imagine, either. A complete mystery," said Mrs. K. Her sly look reminded me that Dad had said she used to work for the city, and, of course, she took all kinds of photographs.

Scully stopped just short of the ramp and slapped the deed on the seat next to him. "With what's left of this, we'll plan our next job. A new assignment is that which the long arm of Oobarab seeks now," he said. Then, scratching his bony chin, he looked off into the distance of the pines as if he could see for miles.

"For me alsho," said Mr. Stimp, nudging his very tall companion in the side. "We need to shtretch out. Find what'sh new."

"Und now ve go!" said the German. "Auf viedersehen, kinder!"

"Toodles!" said Marcia Chalmers, smiling and waving her purple veil.

With that, the sedan spun half a squishy doughnut and shrieked away. I wondered whether I would see that beat-up old car or its passengers ever again. After all that had happened, I hoped I would.

When Mrs. K, Chester Dobbs, Dia, and I walked through the front doors, the nurses at the desk barely raised their heads. "Hey, Dobbsy," they chimed, and waved us right in.

All during the short elevator ride, my stomach was doing flip-flops. Emerson Beale! Alive! What would he be like, after all? I knew who he was now. Dia was right about me hoping for it. But I had yet to even whisper the word to myself.

I think Dobbs, Mrs. K, and Dia hung back as we approached his room because this was special for me. I looked at each of them, then pushed the wide door open and walked in.

Gandy Bridge, Six Miles Long, Between Tampa and St. Petersburg, Florida

P-106

CHAPTER FORTY-THREE

There he was: a man as thin as a stick, his clothes hanging off him, a few wisps of white hair combed across his mottled white head. He was propped up in a chair by the window, surrounded by pillows, connected to monitors and IV drips, slowly tapping the keys of a laptop. He stopped for a moment to look out the window, and I wondered if he had seen the blue sedan in the driveway.

I breathed out. "Mr. Beale . . . Nick . . . sir . . ."

He turned, and a white face stared at me, one eyelid closed. He was wrinkled and weathered and smaller in a way I hadn't imagined from the stories. I could see what I thought were the scars of his war wounds lining his cheeks and jaw and around his eyes, whitened beyond white, but maybe those were just the signs of age. I wasn't sure anymore if that part of the story were true. It seemed then as if a light went on inside of him.

"You're Jason," he said in a low voice, straining to smile.

I could sense Dia in the hall behind me. I felt a sob in my throat, but kept it down. "Yes."

"You found the postcards."

"Uh-huh." I pulled the first one from the Hotel DeSoto from my pocket. He laid the computer on the bed and took it from me.

"I sent this to your grandmother to tell her I was still alive," he said, as if the big story was right there on the tip of his tongue. "An old mystery writer's trick —"

"My trick, if anyone's listening," Dobbs grumbled from the hall.

Emerson held the card up to the ceiling light, ran his fingers over the little twinkle of light as I had done, and made a sound to himself. "I guess I always thought you had to be smart to figure this out."

"Smart?" I said. "I don't know about smart. My mom calls me a smartmouth."

He laughed. It was a bigger, warmer laugh than I would have thought possible from someone so frail and old. It filled the room. "Works for me." He patted the bed. "You must have a lot of questions. Have a seat."

I sat on the edge, catching a glimpse of Dobbs and Dia standing quietly in the hallway now.

"That was some story," I said. "How much . . . was . . . well, I mean, the elephants, the tiger? Was any of it, you know . . ."

"How much was true?" he said with a smile. "I ask myself that question a hundred times a day. Agnes, Marnie, your grandmother — *she* was true. My trying to get to her was true. Now that she's . . ." He trailed off, then started again. "Now that she's gone, I guess it'll be true again, my trying to reach her."

I tried to smile but couldn't. Did he mean he was going to die soon? I wanted to know everything. I was full of questions, and I began to ask them.

"Why was Fang — her father — so crazy about hiding her, and so crazy about keeping you away?"

329

"Two reasons," he said, as if it pained him to remember them, but also as if he were remembering them all the time. "One is because of the accident."

The first reason, it turned out, was simple. I think. Quincy Monroe and his daughter were flying his experimental helicopter thing. They lost control and crashed into Tampa Bay. She was hurt. Not only in her body, but because of loss of oxygen, in her mind, too. Monroe blamed himself. He had, in fact, caused it, felt guilty, and vowed to spare no expense to help cure her. He took her to clinics all over the world. But even as Emerson Beale told me this, I began to hear the mystery of Nick and Marnie coming out in his words, and to understand the second reason.

The two giant palms that gave the place its name were eerily still. The white sands spread out before us, then vanished under the black water.

"Nicky," she said, the evening sun kissing, reddening her face before it dropped away into the Gulf. "You n-n-need to know what happened in the autogyro that day."

I pressed her hand palm to palm with mine. "You don't have to tell me," I said.

"I do," she said. "After I got your postcard and read the story in the hotel, and kept coming back to it, I knew I had to find you. My life was empty without you in it. Nothing m-mattered but finding you, Nicky."

My chest heaved. "Marnie..."

"Father refused to hear of it, of course. He forbid me to see you. He would never tell me why until that day in his autogyro. I demanded he explain it to me. Daddy said your father...your father suspected that he ch-cheated him and others. Of millions. That Daddy destroyed their savings, everything they had. He said you meant trouble. You would discover the truth. We argued, fought terribly. I said things. Daddy...struck me. He couldn't believe he had d-d-done it. Then, as if he saw n-no other way out, he let go of the controls. I screamed. Nick, the gyro plunged. We hit the Bay hard. The crash threw me, they say. I don't remember. My spine was... damaged. I was under the water for a long time." She turned to me. "Thinking about you, of course. What else was I going to do?"

She laughed then. I cried and kissed her.

"Nick, I was under for three minutes. Only you, your face..." She held my cheeks in her hands and kissed me. "You kept me alive in my watery tomb."

Marnie breathed in the blue air, saying nothing for a while. "I was in a coma. Four months. Daddy survived, but seeing me there, knowing he was to blame, he vowed to spend his whole empire for me. He hated you,

tooth—blamed you for poisoning me against him, for trying to take me away, for being who you were, tied to
his...his...crimes. Daddy was a lonely man. His mind
turned d-dark that day over the Bay, Nick. As black as
swamp water."

I held her.

There was nothing more I could do but hold her.

Nothing.

Slowly, the hospital room formed around us again. My
cheeks were wet. "So that's why Monroe hated you so
much? Because of your father?"

"Hate?" he said. "I don't know what it was, but I don't
think it was hate. It was something inhuman. My father
had mortgaged everything to buy a few hundred acres. For
us, for our future, he told my mother. He held onto them
after the collapse of the land boom, held on through the
Depression, hoping their value would come back, only to
find everything stolen from him in one of Monroe's land
grabs. His heart couldn't take it. My father died not ten
yards from the big house on Beach Drive, planning to do
who knows what. Monroe knew that there were a thousand Raymond Beales out there, men like my father who
lost everything, and he feared that if I got too close to the

family, his vast web of swindles would be exposed. Knowing what kind of person he was only made me want to take Marnie away from him sooner. Being with your grandmother was like . . . Jason, you wouldn't believe how truly beautiful she was."

"I read the story. I can guess."

He searched my face, then lowered his voice so I had to lean closer. "There was a scandal," he said. "Your grandmother and I. We finally did get together. That part of the story wasn't made up. Her spine was damaged in the accident, but she could bear a child, and did. Your father."

And I knew it. A lump grew in my throat. "So . . . you . . . really are . . . my grandfather?"

His hand, cold as it was, took mine and held it tight. "Yes, Jason. If I did anything right at all, it was loving your grandmother. She was Marnie, of course, but so much more. She was *alive.*"

I liked hearing about her as she was so many years ago. It was like those postcards. As Randy said, they showed you things that weren't there anymore. But in a way, that made them seem more real. Nick and Marnie's story was like that, too. There was something beautiful, magical about the two of them together. I couldn't think of

Grandma and Emerson without thinking about the story, and the story drove me right back to thinking about them. If I was confusing the two, everyone else seemed to have, also. It was almost impossible not to.

Taking a breath, his chest heaved and calmed. "By the time your dad was in school, Monroe was a sick man, nearly penniless himself, having spent millions on her treatments. In his darkness of mind, he sent for me. I went to him."

Fang heaved himself down behind the desk in his office at the Hotel DeSoto, as dusty and funereal now as Miss Havisham's wreck of a parlor. He was long out of the big house now, out of nearly everything, while Marnie was in Austria, or was it Peru? Burma? In a few minutes, it wouldn't matter where.

He scanned me with that hole of an eye socket, then opened his cigarette case and pulled out a folded postcard. "She never saw this," he murmured. "What does it mean? What do they all mean?"

I stared at the fat man, his face pouring sweat off it like a wax dummy in the sun. Only there wasn't any sun. Everything was dark. We were dark, too. I said nothing.

He leaned forward and told me point-blank: "A doctor has surfaced. Another doctor. Marnie has little left as it is, but may die unless she gets to his clinic in Tokyo."

"You're mad. You're the one who's killing her. She'll die with you hovering over her, caging her in," I said. "She needs to fly away from you and your...your prison —"

He bared his teeth. His fat hand reached back as if to haul off and clock me one. But he let it fall. His face fell, too. With the weight of sorrow drawing him down, he began to talk. "You don't know what it's like. Her mind...every day...the damage is worse. She lost her heart, her memories, because of that accident. She doesn't know you anymore —"

"She does," I said.

"Her mind...," he repeated, then stopped, as if telling me any more would exhaust him. His one eye began to weep.

Fang seemed nearly human then.

"Soon, there will be nothing left," he continued, panting with every move of his hands. "Neither of this dynasty, nor of me. Nor of Marnie, unless I do something —"

"Your dynasty was the cause of the argument in the

autogyro," I said. "It was the cause of Marnie's inju-
ries, and now you've lost it all to pay for your crimes.
Ironic, isn't it?"

"Soon, I will be dead," he said, ignoring me. "Sleeping the big sleep. I want you — *you* — to promise me you'll
continue her treatments when I'm gone."

"Me?"

He groaned in his throat. "I can't trust my own smart
lawyers. Their noses smell only money. I need someone ...
someone who will not fail to pay the ravenous bills for
her care."

"How can I do that?" I said. "I'm only a writer."

"With this."

He pulled open a drawer and slid his hands in. It
wasn't a gun he pulled out, but a couple of sheets of
paper.

"What is it?" I asked.

His face was pale like frozen fish.

"You talk of ironies?" he said. "It's a deed to land
more valuable than your father ever dreamed of. The income is more than enough to care for her after I die.
Take care of that ... love child of yours, too, but especially my daughter. My Marnie!"

While he wept, I picked up the deed and read it. The
land under the Gandy Bridge on both sides was his,

leased to the county. No wonder Oobarab was going to tie me under the bridge. It was their backyard. The income from the lease brought millions. It would pay for Marnie, and for our son.

But the terms of the deed were pure Fang.

Human? My father was right. He had no soul. No heart at all beat in that fat chest.

"Why? What did it say?" I asked him.

Emerson shifted in his chair. Night had fallen on the city behind him.

"The deed forbade me to have any contact with Marnie or our son," he said. "If I did, his lawyers would release false documents about crimes I was supposed to have commited. I would be jailed, the deed would be canceled, and your grandmother would be thrown without a cent on the mercy of the state. The same would happen if I married her, even after he died. Not only that, it committed me to silence about his crimes. If and when she died, the land would become the property of the Order of Oobarab."

"They told us it belonged to them now," I said.

"In this way," he went on, "Monroe's terrible hatred

would continue after his death. His lawyers on one side, vigilant to the suspicion and contempt he had for me, Oobarab always watching me on the other. I guess I was weak, I should have fought it, but I loved your grandmother, saw her ebbing away every day, and I felt I had no choice. He trusted no one, but in a strange way, he trusted me. Whatever else he thought, he knew I loved her. So I had to let her go, and your father along with her."

Laughing, Fang watched me sign the deed, then put his fat palm out.

"It is done," he said.

When I didn't take his hand, he grabbed mine, opened its palm and slapped his on it, as if sharing blood with me. "Palms together, twins in our pact!"

I staggered to my feet, the devil's deed in one hand, his sweaty palm in the other.

He laughed a cold laugh, flicking his eyes at the papers that burned my fingers. "You don't know how sick it makes me to give that to you...you..."

He turned away, too disgusted to speak another word. And I realized that as much as he loved his daughter, he despised me more.

The room came back to us. "Year after year went by. Marnie spent seven years in Tokyo. The old man clung to life into his nineties. His agents got old with him."

"They're back together again, maybe to stay," I said, and he seemed to like that. "But why did you hide the deed? Was the Secret Order after you?"

He shook his head slowly. "Not them. As long as I had the deed in my possession, Marnie had the care she needed. When the old man died, it was his lawyers I feared most. If they got hold of the deed, they would fix it so that they no longer needed me. For my own safety, and for your grandmother's, I hid it."

Dobbs grunted faintly from the hallway. "Or, rather, I did."

Emerson smiled in agreement. "When Monroe died twenty years ago, it was nearly too late, anyway. Your grandmother was hurt in that accident in ways I couldn't guess until years after. She had lost her way. I was half blind, my heart and lungs failing me. Your father — it tore my heart in two to keep the secret from him. I took chances. I decided to become Fred Fracker again, a lawyer friend of his mother's. I got closer. As time wore on, I said things. That Walter Huff wasn't real. That if he ever got a postcard, it meant he was loved, *loved*. But your father . . . he never trusted me. Finally, he told me to go away and never come back. He was hurt, angry at the way his life was being treated. He said he had to move on. I never told him. Never . . ."

He began to cry then, and we sat quietly for a while.

"If I couldn't see her, I could write about her and to her. Words became everything to us. Finally, that's all we had, the story. If Marnie and I lived at all, it was there. She loved Florida. When she no longer got out in it, I made a Florida for her. Of the mind, you could say."

My heart beat faster at that. "I think I know what you mean."

"Even that stopped," he said. "Life went on. Your grandmother's light grew dimmer. After the lawyers faded from the scene, she and I were finally together, for a few brief months."

"You were? You and Grandma were together again?"

He nodded. "It was heaven, and it was agony, seeing her that way. But it ended when I had to come here. Over the last year, we didn't see each other at all. Now never again. At least a friend of mine looked after her until the end. You know her, of course. Mrs. Keats. Jeanette."

I sat there for a long time, not able to say anything. Hearing it from him, it made a strange kind of sense. But if it made sense between my grandmother and grandfather, I understood, too, how huge the empty space in my father's life was, and had been for years. How much emptier he would be if Mom took me back now.

"When your grandmother died," he said, "Jeanette tried to make sure you and your father found the magazine. Then you both went to see Dobbsy's son-in-law, Randy. I knew the postcard was in the desk, so I asked my old trusty friend here to call you."

I turned to the hallway. "I didn't recognize your voice."

"Face masks are good for lots of things," said Dobbsy.

Emerson smiled. "I always wanted your father to find out this way. But he had his accident, and you followed the trail instead. I sometimes think maybe he's been damaged too much to ever want to know."

"Maybe not," I said. "I think he'd want to know."

"At least you were a good detective."

"I had help," I said.

He glanced into the hall at Dia. "I'm glad you found the card. I'm getting old, and you and your father had to know all of it. Before it goes away with me."

"But the mystery, the chase," I said. "Why did we go through all that?"

He sat quietly for a while, looking off and thinking as if far, far away, and saying nothing. But I guess I already knew why. It was like Heinrich Punch had said. "For ze danger und ze glory." The mystery was the heart of what Nick and Marnie had. *The air was alive with love and danger. So were we.* Of course they were. It was that that kept them going. And that kept us going, too.

He turned to me. "Jason, you followed the trail all the way here. I guess there's nothing to do now but to keep following it."

"Keep following it?" I said. "Where does the story go from here?"

"You're smart. You'll figure it out," he said, starting to cough then. A nurse came in and settled him back into his bed. "Meds time," he said. "When your dad's better, bring him here? We have a lot to talk about." Then, handing back the hotel postcard, he added, "Take care of this."

I said I would, and the nurse asked us to leave.

Chester Dobbs was staying behind, so Mrs. Keats, Dia, and I headed back out the doors when the taxi she had called arrived. Mrs. K went home to sleep and told me that her key would be in the mailbox again — *my* mailbox, which is why I hadn't found it the night before. I told her I'd be back after walking Dia home.

But I never made it. Dia and I stayed up all night in her backyard, talking, then not talking. The sun came up early the next day. No free newspaper.

I called Dad. He said he had been hopping mad at me, ready to call out the Army except that Mrs. Keats had come to see him the day before and told him what a busy little house cleaner I was. Then he said that he had talked to Mom. He sounded rested and stronger. He said he actually would be getting out at noon. I told him I'd be there.

"Uh-huh. And are you *really* going to be here?" he asked.

"Really."

Not even a fraction tired, Dia and I then went back to Grandma's house and neatened it up to be ready for him, saying very little. I expected Becca to come any time, and Randy might be there soon with the first folks looking to buy, though I had my own thoughts about that. I figured I'd better have at least one thing done that Dad had asked me to do, so we walked back to Dia's for the lawnmower.

While she wheeled it from the garage, I stood in her driveway holding the postcard of the Hotel DeSoto.

Nick had said that he and Marnie were really only in the story. Okay. But wasn't it more than that? Weren't we all in the story now, too? Maybe the story was still going on around us, and he lived in it and his friends did, and the Secret Order of Oobarab, and maybe even I did and Dia did, too. It was in the postcards and the places, in the grass and sand and swamps, in the trees and in the air around us. With all these ideas bobbling around inside my brain, I was ready to cry or sigh or laugh or feel some big emotion, but something else happened instead.

Bringing the card slowly up to eye level, I began to shake.

"Dia," I said. "Dia. Dia!"

"I'm adding oil," she said. "What?"

A new pinhole of light twinkled from the picture. It shone from the leftmost lobby window of the hotel like a tiny beacon.

"Nick added a second hole!" I said. "A hole that wasn't here before!"

She grabbed the card from me and held it to the sky.

Her face lit up like a sun. "Holy crikey and a half! The last chapter of the story! It's at the hotel! We have to go there!"

"They're tearing it down today —"

But she was already running to the house yelling, "Mommy, Mommy! We need a ride!"

CHAPTER FORTY-FOUR

We didn't stop to eat or go to the bathroom, but we did stop and drag Randy Halbert from his icy office, and were still at the Hotel DeSoto in eighteen minutes. I could give you a play-by-play, but mostly it was Randy who knew everyone, since he was Mr. Real Estate and was part of the mall going up there. We found out he could bend the truth pretty well, too. He told everyone that Dia and I needed five minutes alone to take pictures for a photographic history project.

Not a lot of time, but a chance to find the end of the story.

Using the new pinhole on the postcard, we searched

around the giant left window inside the lobby. The glass wasn't there but something Dia called a cornice was, which was a long narrow box over the window behind which all the curtain works were hidden.

We stacked junk high and climbed onto the thing and searched. After only a minute and a half, Dia found it. Snugged inside the uppermost part of the decoration on top of it was a single piece of paper. She unfolded it slowly, looking at me the whole time.

"The end," she said. "My gosh, Jason, I'm shaking."

I wondered at first how anything could still be there after the way the hotel was torn apart, but when I saw the words I knew it hadn't been there very long. It was done on a computer.

"Dobbsy hid this," said Dia, smiling. "Like . . . this morning."

We jumped down into the dust without reading it. Just before we left, I took as many pictures as I could, including one of Dia at the bottom of the stairs, holding the final page of Emerson Beale's story like a prize.

The lobby shimmered in the light reflected from the building opposite, and I felt the heat again as I hadn't for a while. I was sticky in my shirt. I loved it.

When Randy called from the door — "Time's up, guys. Really." — Dia and I thanked him, then went to the diner across the street, where we sat for the next hour, reading that one page over and over and over. I was crying by the end of it. So was Dia.

Twin Gandy Bridges, across Tampa Bay between
Tampa and St. Petersburg, Florida

CHAPTER FORTY-FIVE

— V —

A FLORIDA OF THE MIND

By Emerson Beale

The sun came up on the beach that first morning under
wild palms, and the next morning, and the one after
that, too. Our lives were magic.

For a few weeks.

But no matter what she said or did or how she smiled
at me, Marnie couldn't last long without her doctors.
She was fading.

Whether Fang was the devil of a soulless ghost I'd

always thought he was, or just a father torn apart by guilt and pain, didn't matter anymore. Marnie was slipping away from me, day by day, week by week.

They say you're whole again when you fly up to heaven. Just maybe, I thought, you can be whole again in a story, too. If we couldn't be together in life, we could be together there. There it was always Nick and Marnie. Marnie and Nick. Just a little story of a girl trying to fly and a bad man trying to hold her down and a guy running through Hades to save her. That's the way that story went. That's the way it keeps on going.

After a while, the story was all we had.

But that was plenty. The more I looked, the more I found it all around me.

Our story was in the palms swaying wildly in the sea breezes. It was in the alligators moving slowly on the mudbanks, scraping their fat bellies noisily into the water... *scooo* ... *splash*.... It was in the sound of insects whirring at twilight and in the hovering blur of hummingbirds.

It was in the way moss hangs from low branches; the thick, greeny smell of it, and how sometimes when you walk under its tendrils in the early blue morning they touch your face with a damp coolness, but you don't wipe it away because that would break the charm.

It was in people, too, living people, who carry it in
their own lives so that the charm never breaks.
It has a name, that charm we have.
Florida.

So that was everything. The last word. We must have
read that page fifty times without leaving the booth. My
heart was heavy and full and coming apart in my chest,
but it felt about as good and right as anything ever had.
And I knew that if I hadn't felt something then, I would
never feel anything ever. Across the table from me, Dia's
eyes were wet. I wanted to reach out to her, or do something. I don't even know what I wanted other than not to
be anywhere else in the world.

A big commotion came then, and all the trucks moved
out. We couldn't have gotten near the hotel if we'd wanted
to. The cranes came in, the wrecking balls swung, and the
Hotel DeSoto came down in crash after crash of cinder
blocks and dust.

"He saw her there first," said Dia, watching the plumes
of dust rise straight up. "There's just the postcard now."

We left the diner. It was still early. Dia said we could
walk partway to the hospital and be there before ten, so

Mrs. Martin drove us for a bit, then went on ahead while we zigagged through the streets the rest of the way.

"This first postcard," I said as we waited for a light to change.

"What about it?"

"It had the tiniest clue, so small and almost invisible, but what if I never saw the hole? Or never found the postcard in the first place? Or if my dad had thrown out the magazine before I saw it? What if we had never gone to the hotel or found the story behind the grate or gone to her old bungalow, or Sunken Gardens, or the Ringling house? What if none of it happened? What would the last few days have been like? We wouldn't be here. The house might be sold. I'd already be back in Boston. Boston!"

The word *empty* came to me again.

Dia looked at me as if she understood something. "Good thing we didn't have to find out."

Dad was waiting in the hospital discharge area with a sad smile on his face. He remembered Dia. She introduced him to her mother, then I wheeled him to the car. By the time we got home, I had finally pulled it all together in my mind. I was going to tell him everything. After all, Dad was one of the most important parts of Marnie and Nick's story.

When we were alone in the house, he propped his leg up on a carton, sank into the couch, looked at me, and shook his head. "Jason, these past few days, I've been doing some thinking —"

I held up my hand, took a deep breath, and started. "Wait, Dad. Before all that stuff, I have to tell you something."

I told him and told him as best I could. Did the story of Emerson Beale and Grandma and Fang and Oobarab make sense? I didn't know anymore. Probably not. Dad asked questions that made it seem full of holes. At first, he was angry at some of it, then I didn't know what he was. His hands were all over his face. He was crying, astonished, crying again, mad. "My father . . . ? Mr. Fracker?"

"Dad, I think it was the only way he could do it. He knows you were mad at him, at everything. But if you could see him you'd know he cares. He always cared. He loves you. He loved Grandma. He still does."

"Oh, man, oh, man," he said softly. "All those years —"

I put the magazine and the typed stories in his lap.

"You didn't lose them," I said. "I mean, not all of them. A lot of it is in the story he wrote. It's right here. And he's still here. Florida is here. And the house."

He cried for a while, softly, then wiped his cheeks as if he remembered something. "You asked me once about postcards. I did get a few, but I only saved one. The first one." He asked for his wallet and opened it. The postcard was folded in half, like the one in Fang's cigarette case. He flattened it and held it out to me.

It was a beach scene of an orange sunset over deep blue water. The awning of a building leaned in from the left side over a railed patio. The description line read, simply:

*Twin Palms Hotel and Beach
Key West, Florida*

In the message area were the words, *I love you.*

Trembling, I gave the card back and said the words to him.

He looked up at me. "I love you, too," he said. Then he shook his head slowly. "Gosh, we've never talked this much."

"You're probably really tired —"

"No. I like it."

I cranked open the back windows. The smell of cut grass drifted into the room, lighting everything up with its fresh scent.

"But I *am* tired," he said.

After a little while of being quiet, he slipped down into the sofa pillows, smiling as his father had when *he* leaned back.

"I'll call the agent later," he said. "For now, I don't know . . ."

I think I did. He drifted off to sleep. I tiptoed out of the room. A few minutes later, my sister Becca called from North Carolina where her flight had a stopover. She said she'd be there in two hours. Fine. Real life was moving in again, but that was okay. After I hung up, I went into my bedroom and stood over the bed where Grandma had had her stroke. It didn't freak me out anymore. That was okay, too. A little later, Hector called. "You'll never guess what," he said.

"You died and came back to life?" I said.

"No . . ."

"You can finally juggle?"

"Still no . . ."

"You're in jail?"

"I'm in Orlando."

"You are?"

"No," he said. "But I will be this weekend. It'll be as hot as a jungle, but we got a deal. Dude, if you're still there, we are so getting together!"

We joked back and forth for a while and made plans for when he came down. But being on the phone with him made me realize that I had to talk to her, too.

Amazingly, Mom was at home, waiting for a limo to take her to the airport to fly here. There was small talk at first, then I said, "Mom, I'm sorry I lied to you."

"Jason —"

"I wouldn't . . . I wouldn't hide anything anymore, Mom. Not anymore."

I heard her breathing softly, just breathing. "Thank you. I know you wouldn't. I know that. I think . . . gosh, this is so hard . . . and it's not like it hasn't been heading toward this for a long time, Jason, but . . . I think your father and I need a break. You know what I mean?"

"I know," I said, surprised at how easily I was able to say

it. "I know. Dad needs somebody. For a while. And I'm here. Maybe, I don't know, I can help him."

"You're not supposed to help him. You're a boy," she said, then was quiet for a while. "But maybe you can. I can't seem to. After the house is sold, if he sells it, then we'll see."

"Maybe just a couple of weeks," I said. "Then we'll see what's going on."

The sun from the backyard was streaming across the kitchen tabletop. I thought I heard someone calling me, but it was birds. We talked for nearly an hour. I told her about Dia, and Hector's trip. It ended this way.

"Maybe I won't come down just now. I'll talk to Daddy later today when he wakes up," she said, "then we can see about how to handle this."

"Okay, Mom. But I think it'll be okay, at least for now." I started to cry then. I tried not to sound like it on the phone at first, but couldn't stop it and cried for minutes.

"Oh, my baby!" she said softly. "I love you, you know."

I breathed in. "We'll do it, Mom. We'll be okay."

"I love you, Jason," she said, more softly still.

"I love you, Mom."

That was good enough for then. After the call, I sat for a few minutes, but the sound of birds kept me from getting too deep into myself then. I went to the sink and washed my face, then out the back door to the patio. Dia was raking up the lawn cuttings into piles and humming. It had been a while between mowings.

I watched her work for a minute or two, running over what I had told Dad, and I kept coming back to what she had said once. Maybe it couldn't happen, but it could still happen. I thought then how we all have stories. Sometimes they're so short you could fit them onto the back of a postcard.

I think we need a break.

Other times they're so long they take a lifetime to write before they're finished. And sometimes everything that happens is connected to everything else that happens, and the stories are so big and long and deep they never finish. I liked that kind the best.

Finally, I stopped thinking and just watched Dia raking piles in the yard. She might have sensed I was watching, but she didn't say anything. I went over to her.

"So . . . ," I said.

"So," she repeated. "What?"

"So . . . I think maybe we'll stay for a while."

Not raising her head from the back-and-forth work of her rake, she smiled. "Yeah, you will."

THE END